When Steven opened his eyes again, he was facing the row directly behind Ferris's—where, sitting all by herself, was Jill Hale. The girl he'd had the hots for before Cathy came along.

His heart gave a leap. Jill was just as beautiful as he'd remembered her being. No. More. He shut his eyes again, remembering how he used to feel about Jill, remembering how hard he'd tried to get to know her, remembering how happy he'd been when she'd agreed to go out with him that one time. And after going out with Cathy for so long, maybe he needed just a little change. Nothing against Cathy, of course. Just that he needed a little oomph. A little extra. A little Jill Hale.

Jill's eyes flicked away from the screen. He gripped the back of Ferris's chair tightly. He could hardly breathe—Jill was looking directly at him, smiling, he could have sworn it!

And if he moved all the way down to the end of Ferris's row, he'd be right in front of Jill. Steven's mouth was drier than ever. His palms wouldn't quit sweating. He knew he probably should be getting back to Cathy, but how could he turn away from Jill?

Almost without knowing what he was doing, he began climbing over legs to the end of the row.

SWEET VALLEY TWINS

Big Brother's in Love Again

◇

Written by
Jamie Suzanne

Created by
FRANCINE PASCAL

BANTAM BOOKS
NEW YORK · TORONTO · LONDON · SYDNEY · AUCKLAND

To David Johänn Boulton

RL 4, 008-012

BIG BROTHER'S IN LOVE AGAIN
A Bantam Book / February 1997

*Sweet Valley High® and Sweet Valley Twins® are
registered trademarks of Francine Pascal.*

Conceived by Francine Pascal.

*Produced by Daniel Weiss Associates, Inc.
33 West 17th Street
New York, NY 10011.*

Cover art by Bruce Emmett.

ISBN: 0-553-48435-4

Published simultaneously in the United States and Canada

Bantam Books are published by Bantam Books, a division of Bantam
Doubleday Dell Publishing Group, Inc. Its trademark, consisting of the
words "Bantam Books" and the portrayal of a rooster, is Registered in the
U.S. Patent and Trademark Office and in other countries. Marca
Registrada. Bantam Books, 1540 Broadway, New York, New York 10036.

PRINTED IN THE UNITED STATES OF AMERICA

OPM   0 9 8 7 6 5 4 3 2 1

One

◇

"You're going to the dance, right?" Amy Sutton asked Elizabeth Wakefield. It was Friday at lunch, and the two friends were sitting in the cafeteria at Sweet Valley Middle School, where they were both in the sixth grade.

Elizabeth swallowed her mashed potatoes and wondered how she should answer the question. "I think so," she said doubtfully. "That is—"

"That is, what?" Amy asked, frowning.

Elizabeth plastered a smile on her face. "That is, nothing," she answered slowly. She was sure she'd have a blast at the upcoming Valentine's Day street dance. She could see herself now, gliding along the pavement in the arms of Todd Wilkins, her sort-of boyfriend, while the band played.

There was only one small problem. Todd hadn't

officially asked her yet. In fact, Todd hadn't asked her at all, officially or unofficially. And the dance was only a week away. "Is Ken taking you?" she asked Amy. Ken Matthews, one of Todd's closest friends, was Amy's sort-of boyfriend.

Amy bit her lip. "Well—" She pushed her apple cobbler around with a fork. "I hope so," she said in a small voice, "but he hasn't exactly asked me."

Elizabeth was sorry for her friend, but she couldn't help feeling a little relieved. *At least I'm not the only one*, she thought. "Um—that's too bad."

"Did Todd ask you yet?" Amy asked.

"No." Elizabeth wrinkled her nose. "But it's not like I'm worried or anything," she added defensively. "Todd always waits till the last minute. He just kind of assumes I'm available."

"Same with Ken," Amy said. She smiled at Elizabeth. "So I'm not, like, worried or anything either," she said.

Elizabeth couldn't help thinking that her friend didn't sound that convincing. She forced a careless laugh. "I just wonder if something's going on," she said aloud. *Not that there could be anything "going on,"* she assured herself. *Even if Cammi Adams was sort of flirting with Todd during science the other day—*

With a start Elizabeth found she was stabbing her fork into her potatoes. "We could ask *them*, I guess," she suggested. In the corner of the cafeteria she could just make out Todd and Ken, laughing uproariously with a few other boys from the middle-school basketball team. *Good. Cammi's nowhere in sight.* Not that she really *thought* Cammi would be there. She just wanted to be sure.

Amy nodded slowly. "We could," she agreed, brushing a wisp of her long straight hair off her face. "There's no reason in the world why girls can't ask boys places."

"No reason at all," Elizabeth echoed her. *It wouldn't be so hard,* she told herself. She could easily walk over to Todd and Ken's table. She could easily say, "Hey, Todd, want to go to the street dance next week?" *Yeah. No problem.*

Elizabeth licked her lips nervously. *Of course,* she reminded herself, watching Todd elbow Ken in the ribs, *he does look kind of busy just now.* "So, why don't you go ask him?" she said brightly.

"Me?" Amy looked startled. "Well—" Her hands fluttered in the air. "I guess I *could.* It's just that it would be more fun to be asked, you know? But I'll ask Ken if you ask Todd."

Elizabeth considered. She didn't really believe that Todd would ask Cammi. And if she just waited a few days, he'd ask *her.* Wouldn't he? "Nah," she said, flashing Amy what she hoped was a confident smile. "You're right. It'd be more fun to be asked."

"Is Jessica going?" Amy wanted to know.

Elizabeth smiled. "You never can tell with Jess," she said. "But I bet wild horses couldn't keep her away."

Elizabeth and her twin sister, Jessica, were very

different people. Although the twins looked exactly alike, with the same blond hair and blue-green eyes, they were not at all the same on the inside. Elizabeth liked to read, write, and spend time with a few close friends. She took her schoolwork seriously and rarely followed the crowd.

Jessica, on the other hand, lived for fashion, boy talk, parties, and friends. She was a member of the Unicorn Club, a group of girls who considered themselves the prettiest and most popular kids at Sweet Valley Middle School. She thought school was jut a way to pass the time until something better came along.

Elizabeth reached for her cup. She could see Jessica's sort-of boyfriend, Aaron Dallas, sitting at the basketball players' table with Todd and Ken. Had Aaron asked Jessica yet? she wondered just as Winston Egbert swung his long legs over the bench next to Amy.

"Ladies!" Winston Egbert cried. Elizabeth sighed. Winston considered himself the world's greatest stand-up comic. "Caught my gargoyle imitation yet?"

"Your what?" Amy asked blankly.

"My gargoyle imitation," Winston repeated. "You know, gargoyles? Those guys who sit up on top of churches and castles and the rainwater runs out of their mouths onto all the people standing underneath, like spit?" Standing on the bench, he pulled his body into a tight squat.

"If you spit on me, I'll throw my mashed potatoes at you," Amy threatened.

"I won't spit, promise," Winston assured her. "I got the idea watching this incredibly awesome movie about gargoyles coming to life and taking over New Jersey or South Dakota or one of those other states." He bent sharply forward so his face was directly over Elizabeth's tray.

Elizabeth rolled her eyes. She liked Winston, but sometimes he got on her nerves. "Gargoyles are made of stone, Winston. How can you—"

"Hang on, hang on, I've almost got it," Winston interrupted. He spread out his fingers and twisted his arms into what Elizabeth suspected was a very uncomfortable position. "The trick's in the muscles," he added. Grinning, he crossed his eyes and stuck his tongue out a few inches. Then he held perfectly still for a second. "Pretty cool, huh?"

Amy shuddered. "That's totally disgusting, Winston."

"Hey, thanks!" Winston popped up and stretched his arms back as far as they would go. "I've been practicing all week. Want to see another one?"

Elizabeth took a deep breath. "Actually, Winston, could you find somebody else to—" *To bug*, she was going to say, but she stopped, worried about hurting Winston's feelings.

"Okeydokey." Winston jumped down from the bench. "You'll have another chance to see me next week. In my first, ahem—*live* performance." He shined his fingernails on his shirt.

"Your first what?" Amy made a face.

"My first live performance," Winston repeated proudly. "You know. At the Valentine's dance? The organizers asked me to come up with a little, um, light entertainment."

"You?" Elizabeth asked, then bit her lip. "I mean—"

"Sure, me," Winston said with a shrug. "I'm the funniest guy in the school, in case you hadn't noticed. And I'm not going to sing and dance, that's definitely out. 'Oh, Winston!'" he said in a silly voice, kneeling and staring into the air with a wistful expression, "'would you kindly consent to dance and sing for us next Friday? You could do ballet, tap, modern, or even the bunny hop!'"

Elizabeth chuckled. She had to admit, Winston could be funny all right. And the idea of Winston in a tutu . . . Catching Amy's eye, she saw that her friend was grinning too.

"Yup, that's what the organizers said to me," Winston went on. He stood and dusted off his knees. "But I said no. Since I intend to be the first performing artist to do a one-man gargoyle show when I grow up, or even before, I'll do my imitations on the curb. There'll be a hat out front for, um, *donations*." He stared meaningfully at the girls. "It's just too bad about the basketball team," he murmured with a sigh.

"The basketball team?" Amy frowned. "What about them?"

"Haven't you heard?" Winston blinked his eyes rapidly and put on a soulful expression. "Dead," he said. "The whole SVMS basketball team. Killed in the volcano explosion of '63."

"Oh, please." Elizabeth shook her head. "Can't you be serious for once? What *about* the basketball team?" She looked across at Todd and the other members of the team. The odds were that Winston was just blowing steam, but you never could tell with Winston.

"You mean you don't know about the away game the day of the dance?" Winston said in mock horror. He put an imaginary microphone to his mouth. "Winston Egbert reporting to you live from the SVMS cafeteria, where I'm talking with the only two students airheaded enough not to know about the game that conflicts with the Valentine's Day dance—"

"Oh, cut it out," Elizabeth snapped. She resented being called an airhead. But that wasn't the only thing Winston said that made her feel uncomfortable. "What time does the bus get back?" she asked.

Winston gave a short barking laugh. "Like, late. Like, the crack of dawn. Too late for the dance anyway," he added gloomily. "A team bus and, I don't know, two fan buses, and, like, three quarters of the guys in the whole school. Can you imagine? They'd rather watch a dumb basketball game than me, the greatest living interpreter of gargoyle culture worldwide?" Without waiting for an answer, he shot his arms out, bent from the waist, and twisted his mouth into an awkward scowl that made his neck muscles stand out.

Elizabeth bit her lip. "Uh-oh," she said to Amy.

"You can say that again," Amy sighed. "If the bus doesn't get back till real late, then—" She slumped next to her tray. "Looks like neither of us has a date for the dance."

"Maybe they'll skip the game," Elizabeth said hopefully. "Maybe Ken and Todd will decide the dance is more important."

"Maybe," Amy said, not sounding at all convinced.

"Hey, look!" Winston cried, but Elizabeth ignored him. She wasn't convinced herself. *Todd sure loves basketball*, she thought as the team members got up from the table across the room. *I can't imagine him missing a game, even for a dance. Even for—*

She swallowed hard.

Even for me.

"I guess we should ask them just to make sure," Amy said with a sigh. "I mean, you never know, right?"

"Stranger things have happened," Elizabeth agreed. But she couldn't think of anything stranger than Todd sacrificing a basketball game for her.

"Hey!" Winston spun around. "Was that cool, or what?" he boasted, flexing his fingers to make sure the blood was still flowing. "I call that pose Goyle. Like, Gar and Goyle, get it? Get it?"

Amy squeezed her eyes shut tight. "Would you leave us alone, please?" she asked him.

Winston shrugged. "Hey, you know me," he said. "Always happy to oblige." Saluting smartly, he turned—and smacked right into Todd and Ken. "Oof!" he groaned, sliding to the floor and holding his head in apparent pain.

Todd looked at the floor. "You all right, Egbert? Need a doctor or something?" He bent down to offer Winston a hand.

"No, no, it's OK," Winston gasped, rolling from side to side on the floor. "I need to practice my—death scenes. Ohhhhh—" He closed his eyes theatrically and made a horrible rasping sound in his throat. "Promising young talent struck down in the—wheeze—prime of life—"

Elizabeth tried to ignore him. "Hi, Todd," Elizabeth said shyly. She wondered what he and Ken were doing over here anyway. "Um—how are you?"

"Water—gasoline—ammonia—" Winston coughed, wriggling away like a snake in a desert. "Must have water—gasoline—ammonia—"

"Fine," Todd said, straightening up. "We came to invite you guys someplace next week."

"You did?" Elizabeth shot Amy a hopeful look. So Todd *was* going to stick around for the street dance! She *knew* Valentine's Day was more important to him than some game.

"The away game against Glenwood," Todd explained.

Elizabeth felt her heart drop.

"The game?" Amy asked weakly.

Todd nodded eagerly. "There's, like, three fan buses going—"

"Four," Ken interjected. "They just added another one."

"Four," Todd agreed, "and the game's going to be a classic. Like, slaughter city. We're going to clobber them."

"Murder them," Ken added happily.

"Cream them," Todd suggested.

"Blow them away!" Ken said, pumping his fists. "But those fan buses are, like, filling up fast. We didn't want you to be left out in the cold."

Elizabeth had trouble finding her voice. "But how about the street dance?" she asked.

"We thought you'd take us to the dance that night," Amy said.

"Oh, the dance." Todd shrugged. "We can go dancing some other time."

Ken nodded. "But it's not every day you get to see Matthews and Wilkins in action." He wadded up a napkin from Amy's tray. "Matthews shoots the three!" he announced, tossing it into Amy's cup of milk.

"Gee, thanks," Amy said sarcastically, pulling the napkin out. "I wasn't exactly done with the milk yet."

Ken seemed not to notice. "The bus sign-up's on the bulletin board next to the gym," he said, turning to leave. "Be there—"

"Or beware," Todd finished, chuckling. "See you around!" Together they walked off, laughing.

Elizabeth tightened her mouth as she watched her so-called boyfriend leave the cafeteria.

Todd's invitation hadn't been exactly the one she'd had in mind.

Jessica scowled and steered the shopping cart carefully around the waxed eggplant display in the supermarket. No way was she letting anybody think her family might eat disgusting, gross vegetables like that. Her mouth watered for ice cream, cola, and croissants fat with chocolate raspberry filling—

"I think we'll need three of those," her mother said, pointing to the eggplants. "No, make that four. They're for the eggplant-spinach casserole Sunday night."

Jessica tried her best not to gag. "Remind me to eat someplace else Sunday night," she said, throwing the four smallest eggplants she could find into a bag.

It was after school on Friday afternoon, and Jessica had been roped into helping her mother with the weekly marketing. She hated grocery shopping. Her mother always embarrassed her to death. She'd linger by the Pepto-Bismol display, or she'd buy tons of cans of something vomitrocious like corned beef hash. Jessica closed the eggplant bag and tossed it into the cart. "Oh, Mom, you didn't get mushroom soup again!" she groaned.

Mrs. Wakefield gave Jessica a tight smile. "Your father and I happen to like mushroom soup," she said patiently.

Yeah, well, you would, Jessica thought. She leaned against the shopping cart and gently kicked a display case. "And what's with the six gallons of milk?" she demanded.

Mrs. Wakefield stared a little above Jessica's head. "They're half gallons. And mostly they're for your brother. Steven drinks a lot because—"

"Because he's a pig," Jessica muttered under her breath. Her brother, a freshman at Sweet Valley High, ate everything in sight. Every time Jessica saw Steven, he was busy stuffing his face.

"What did you say?" Mrs. Wakefield frowned and reached for a box of prunes.

Jessica cringed. "Nothing," she said sweetly.

"Oh." Mrs. Wakefield fixed her with a look. "Steven needs plenty of milk right now because it's basketball season. He burns up lots of calories."

Basketball season. Great. Jessica didn't want to think about basketball season right now. Not after what Aaron Dallas had done to her this afternoon. Aaron Dallas, her used-to-be sort-of boyfriend, who had abandoned her when she needed a date for the street dance just so he could go play a stupid basketball game. And hadn't even sounded sorry about it.

He could have sent me flowers or something, she

thought glumly. But instead, Aaron had only said, "A man's gotta do what a man's gotta do," and then he'd burst into hysterical laughter. Jessica straightened up and shoved the cart forward angrily. *Some great romance*, she thought. *Give weeks of your life to the guy, and he won't even take you out on Valentine's Day. Some great—*

"And this is my daughter Jessica," Mrs. Wakefield was saying.

Jessica looked up. *Oops.* She'd almost run the cart over the foot of a woman in a purple sweater. "Hi," Jessica said, scowling, and then looked back down at the ground.

"This is Mrs. Claybaugh," Mrs. Wakefield said. "Pete's mother. Remember Pete Claybaugh, Steven's friend? They're on the basketball team together?"

Basketball. That word again. Jessica nodded as noncommittally as possible and stared at the display in front of her. Dried beans. Ugh. She'd always hated dried beans. She hoped this would be a short conversation.

Mrs. Wakefield sighed and raised her eyebrows. "She's twelve, you know," she told Mrs. Claybaugh, as though that explained everything.

Jessica set her jaw. She hated being talked about as if she weren't there. But what would you expect from someone who actually *liked* mushroom soup?

"I know exactly what you mean!" Mrs. Claybaugh said with feeling. "Pete's cousins are visiting from out of town. Their school's off for a little while. One's in sixth and the other's in seventh, and talk about difficult! Well—"

Cousins. Jessica hadn't known Pete had cousins. She probably wouldn't like them very much, she decided, studying the label on the dried lima beans. A picture sprang into her mind: two girls, one blond and short, one dark and tall, each with freckles and a turned-up nose. One would be like Elizabeth, Jessica decided, down-to-earth and serious and kind of unsophisticated, and the other would be like her friend Lila, who was fun to be with but could be kind of demanding sometimes. She ran her hand down the edge of the shopping cart. Well, it didn't matter anyway. She wasn't going to worry about a couple of girls who were just visiting.

"—and the mess in the bathroom after they shower! Let me tell you!" Mrs. Claybaugh said.

Jessica sighed. Her thoughts drifted back to Aaron. Aaron, who she'd thought was so great. Aaron, who she'd have walked through fire for. Well. Maybe not through *fire*. But through a room without air-conditioning anyway.

"If they were girls, I'd invite them over to meet the twins," Mrs. Wakefield said. She took the handle of the shopping cart. "Enjoy your nephews, showers and all! Take care, Barbara."

If they were girls? Jessica started in surprise. *Nephews?* She followed her mother out of the aisle, suddenly realizing that Pete's cousins weren't girls at all. "Actually, Mom," she began, her head whirling with all kinds of thoughts, "even if they aren't girls they could still come over."

Mrs. Wakefield stopped by a display of sanitary napkins and frowned. "What are you talking about, Jessica?"

"Pete's nephews," Jessica explained. "I mean, Mrs. Claybaugh's nephews. Pete's *cousins*. They could come over. If they wanted to." The freckle-faced girls with the turned-up noses disappeared, to be replaced by a couple of really cute guys. Drop-dead gorgeous. Johnny Buck's looks with Arnold Weissenhammer's muscles. And Aaron Dallas's smile . . .

No, scratch that, she told herself. *Forget Aaron Dallas. As of now, he just might be history.*

"They're only here for a week, Jessica," Mrs. Wakefield said. "Just till their vacation ends. Should we buy the large economy size on the sanitary napkins, or—"

Jessica sighed. In her mind the Claybaugh brothers were tall and dark, suave and debonair. Athletic too, but not into skipping dances for stupid basketball games. No. These guys would skip the Olympics if Jessica gave the word. She grinned.

"Jes-si-ca!" Mrs. Wakefield's voice rang in her ears. "I asked you to hand me that box, please!"

As Jessica reached for the box, two of the coolest-looking boys she had ever seen came darting around the corner, clutching skateboards. They were drop-dead gorgeous. She drew in her breath.

"Aunt Barbara!" the boys yelled. "Aunt Barbara!"

The Claybaugh cousins! Jessica's eyes grew wide. Of course! Her mom had called Mrs. Claybaugh 'Barbara,' right? And the two guys looked the right age to be the sixth- and seventh-grade nephews from out of town.

"Jessica, please." Mrs. Wakefield tapped her foot impatiently.

Jessica stole a quick glance toward the bean aisle. She had to meet the boys. She couldn't let this opportunity go by, could she?

Of course not!

"Oh, darn!" she said, slapping the side of her head and looking at her mother with the most winning smile she could manage. "I forgot to get the dried beans—and you know how much I love dried beans!"

Mrs. Wakefield widened her eyes. "Since when do you—"

But Jessica was already on the move.

Two

◇

"Mo-om!" Jessica rolled her eyes for what felt like the eighty-third time since they'd arrived in the store.

"Oh, I'm sorry!" Mrs. Wakefield apologized, taking her credit card out of the slot at the checkout counter. "Silly me. I ran it through the slot upside down."

"Won't work that way, ma'am," the checkout clerk said. He was a tall man with a cheerful grin that made Jessica want to puke. She hoped he wouldn't offer her a lollipop.

On the other hand, being offered a lollipop would be the perfect cap to an awful day. First there was Aaron, Aaron the Obnoxious. Then she'd missed Pete's cousins. They'd been skateboarding across the parking lot by the time she got back to the bean aisle. Finally, Mrs. Wakefield decided to use dried beans in three dinners next week, since Jessica liked them so much all of a sudden.

The clerk looked at Jessica as Mrs. Wakefield slid the card through again. "What's the matter, young lady?" he asked. "No boyfriends?"

Jessica stared at the man in surprise, wondering how he knew.

The checkout man smiled widely. "That's OK," he said, tearing off the receipt and handing it to Mrs. Wakefield to sign. "You'll break some poor guy's heart when you're older. And by the way," he added in a whisper. "Keep it under your hat, but there were these two good-looking young men racing around with skateboards a while back."

Jessica edged away. "Uh-huh," she said.

"Thanks a lot, ma'am," the clerk said, accepting the signed receipt from Mrs. Wakefield. "You have a nice day, OK? You too," he said to Jessica, winking at her. "Take my advice, miss, keep those two future movie stars to yourself, now. Don't tell your friends! Let 'em be your secret."

Let 'em be your secret. Jessica grinned as she pushed the overloaded cart away from the checkout lane. Suddenly her heart was soaring again. *I'm, like, the only girl in town who knows about those two,* she told herself. *If I play it right, maybe I'll have that date for the dance after all.*

And Aaron Dallas can go eat his basketball shorts!

*   *   *

"So, like, what do you think of Krista Kennedy?" Steven asked, taking a bite of his super-sized sundae. He and his best friend, Joe Howell, were in Casey's ice cream parlor, discussing their second favorite topic after basketball: girls.

Joe shrugged and fiddled with his spoon. "She's pretty hot. Yeah. I guess."

"So why don't you ask her out?" Steven wanted to know. He dug back into his dish, hoping that this little snack would last him the hour or so till dinner.

Joe stretched. "I did, a few weeks ago. We had a good time." He took a swallow from his water glass. "But you gotta understand, man, I'm not like you. I'm not ready to be tied down to just one girl yet. Maybe later." A slow grin spread across his face. "Like when I'm sixty-eight."

Steven sighed. "Going steady's really worth it," he said, thinking of his own girlfriend, Cathy Connors. "You know who you're doing stuff with every Friday night. You've got a date for, like, every dance around. None of this calling two hours before you want to go someplace and getting the runaround. 'Go on a date? With you? Like, tonight?'" he asked in a squeaky voice, pressing an imaginary phone to his ear. "'Oh, I'm sorry, Bo, I mean Joe, I couldn't possibly. I have to stay home and wash my toenails.'" He made a contemptuous sound. "Playing the field. Who needs it?"

Joe shrugged again. "Yeah, you run into some

problems that way," he agreed, "but it's my choice. Freedom, man," he added, tapping his chest meaningfully. "It's the way to go. For me anyway. I'd get tired of the same girl, no matter how hot."

Steven shoveled more ice cream into his mouth. "So you're telling me you don't *want* to be going out with anybody?" he asked.

"You got it." Joe smiled. "You get bored with a girl, you split up. No hard feelings." His eyes followed a couple of girls as they came into Casey's and sat down. "And you can go ask a girl out without making anybody jealous. Like this," he added, standing up slowly and giving Steven a wink.

Steven paused with his spoon halfway to his mouth. He watched Joe straighten his collar and saunter across the room to the table where the two girls sat.

He frowned. Maybe there was something to what Joe said. Sure, Cathy was great. Good-looking. Smart, fun to be with, and a terrific dancer. But maybe Joe's way was best. He stole another look at the two girls at the other table. Joe was standing next to them, arm draped loosely over the taller one's shoulders, grinning away with typical Joe Howell charm.

I couldn't do that, Steven told himself. *Even though I'm taller and handsomer and a better basketball player than Joe.* He bit his lip. The truth was, just flirting with those girls would feel like cheating on Cathy. And he didn't want to be cheating on his steady girlfriend.

On the other hand, even from a distance he could tell that the shorter girl was pretty hot. And it was a shame not to talk to her just because he didn't want to offend Cathy. When she wasn't even here. *And who knows?* he asked himself. The ice cream from the spoon in his hand began to drip onto his blue jeans. *Maybe Joe's right. Maybe I should wait till I'm, like, sixty-eight to settle down with one girl.*

On the *other* other hand, Cathy really was a lot of fun . . . .

Off in the corner, the taller girl giggled and leaned back against Joe's arm. Joe caught Steven's eye and winked again.

Making a face, Steven slid the spoon back into the dish. Suddenly he wasn't so hungry after all.

"So how was school today?" Mrs. Wakefield asked, loading a bag of groceries into the family van.

"Fine," Jessica said, barely listening. *A secret,* she told herself excitedly. The wheels in her head were really spinning now. If she was the only girl in town who knew about these cute boys, then she'd get to be in charge of things. For once.

"How's Lila?" Mrs. Wakefield asked.

"Fine," Jessica replied absently. She scratched her ear, wondering if she should tell Lila and only Lila about the gorgeous cousins. It would be their secret, and they'd show up at the street dance with boyfriends—the only dates for miles around. She grinned. *That would sure show Janet Howell and Kimberly Haver and all those other bossy Unicorns who think they run the earth.* She'd just make Lila promise to never tell a single solitary soul, and make her take the cousin who was a little less good-looking, and—

"That checkout clerk was awfully nice, wasn't he?" Mrs. Wakefield asked, slamming the van door shut.

"Fine," Jessica agreed. *On second thought,* she told herself, *scratch Lila.* Her best friend just wasn't—well, reliable. Jessica could see it now. Lila would swear that she wouldn't tell anyone, but she'd blab, and Lila and Janet would get the boys. Or Lila and Kimberly.

Mrs. Wakefield gave Jessica a searching look. "Did you turn in your book report?"

"Fine," Jessica said, not paying any attention at all. On automatic pilot, she returned the cart and walked back to the van. Maybe she could tell Mandy Miller. Or Mary Wallace. They were probably the nicest Unicorns. *They won't tell if I say it's a secret,* she decided. At least, she didn't think so.

"All set?" Mrs. Wakefield asked.

Jessica nodded, climbed into the passenger seat, and carefully locked her seat belt in place. The problem was, Janet Howell had ways of finding things out. And even somebody nice, like Mary or Mandy, might have a tough time keeping secrets from Janet. So maybe Mary and Mandy weren't the answers either.

She frowned, examining her reflection in the

side-view mirror. Who could she tell who wouldn't blab the news all over town? Who, who, who?

Mrs. Wakefield glanced at her watch and put the car in gear. "I hope someone's home to help put the stuff away," she muttered. "Steven and Elizabeth should both be there by now—"

"Elizabeth!" Jessica sat straight up in the car. She could have cheered. "Hey thanks, Mom!"

"Thanks?" Mrs. Wakefield frowned. "But I didn't—"

Jessica wasn't listening. She stared out the window, a big smile on her face. Elizabeth would be the perfect person to tell about the brothers. *She'd never blab,* Jessica told herself, *and she'll probably take whichever one I don't want.* She could just see Janet sputtering, "But where did you *find* these guys?" And Jessica would toss her head and smile and hook her arm into her gorgeous, suave, debonair date's, and say—and say—

Well, say something really clever that will put Janet in her place anyway.

Jessica leaned back and hummed to herself happily. Who should have first dibs on brothers? Sisters, naturally.

The only problem was, they'd have to move fast. Before somebody else beat them to it.

"So I'll pick her up tomorrow around six, and we'll head out to the mall," Joe said as he returned to Steven's booth. "Her name's Kathleen. I'd tell you the name of her friend, but I know you're kind of committed."

Steven made a face. He hadn't had the guts to go over and talk to the other girl, but he was certain she was trying to flirt with him from across the room. Cathy's face flashed briefly in front of him. He squeezed his eyes shut tight. Sure, Cathy was cute, and fun, and all that stuff, but—

Joe held up a hand. "Oh, don't worry, buddy. I know you're different from me. And you and Cathy are such a great couple, I bet you don't even notice half the hot-looking girls who live in this town." His eyes sparkled.

Oh, boy, are you ever wrong, Steven grumbled to himself. He noticed, all right. He noticed a lot. Hey, there were about a dozen girls right here in Casey's that he'd *noticed*. Not to mention a bunch of other girls in school, and ones he'd met on vacation, and— "Yeah, well, I'm not, you know, blind," he said, running a finger around the edge of his water glass.

Joe looked surprised. "I never said you were. It's just that when you have a steady relationship with someone as cool as Cathy—"

Steven snorted, wadding up his napkin and tossing it into the air. He took a deep breath. *Funny.* Somewhere in the air was a scent that reminded him of the perfume Jill Hale used to wear. Jill had been the last girl he'd dated before going with Cathy full-time. He'd long since gotten over Jill, but he *had* been kind of hot for her at the time . . . .

No. Scratch that. He'd had a *killer* crush on her.

Steven blinked and took another breath. The smell *was* kind of familiar.

"Oh, you'd be crazy not to stick with her," Joe was saying. "But for a guy like me it's different. The open road and all that."

Crazy? Steven knew he should feel flattered. After all, here was his best buddy signing off on his choice of girlfriend. But somehow, he wasn't quite happy. He sniffed the air and tried not to ogle Kathleen's friend too obviously. "I guess you're right," he said at last.

I'm going out with Cathy tonight, he reminded himself. *And she's smart and funny and cool and pretty, and I really really like her a lot, and I don't have to call around to find a date for anything, and it's easy this way and—*

He shook his head.

Somehow, he wasn't doing a very good job of convincing himself.

And he couldn't help feeling that Joe had something that Steven himself didn't.

"I don't see what the big deal is, Jess," Elizabeth said. She munched a celery stick thoughtfully as she put a can of olives into the pantry. "I mean, no one else is going to have a date. And what if we don't even *like* these cousins of Pete's?"

Jessica groaned. "Whether we *like* them or not has absolutely nothing to do with it," she said sternly. "Don't you understand anything?"

Elizabeth sighed. There were times she didn't

even come close to figuring out her sister. "But—" she said.

"Trust me," Jessica interrupted. "It'll be the social coup of the century!"

"What if I don't even *want* to be part of the social coup of the century?" Elizabeth shot back. *Typical Jess,* she thought, *trying hard to put one over on her friends.* "And besides," she added, "I wouldn't feel right about going to the dance with anybody but Todd."

Jessica nodded sagely. "The guy drops you for a stupid basketball game, and you 'wouldn't feel right' about going with some dreamy guy from out of town." She snorted and looked away. "Typical."

"What do you mean?" Elizabeth rummaged through the groceries for the corn chips. "Todd didn't *drop* me. It's just that he really likes basketball. And it's only this one time."

"Ha!" Jessica shot back. She put down a box of lemonade mix and stared fixedly at her sister. "Does Todd *eat* with you? Does he carry your *books?* Does he walk you *home?*"

"Well, no," Elizabeth conceded, feeling a little flustered.

"Does he write you little notes just because?" Jessica went on. "Does he call you on the phone just so he can hear the sound of your voice? Huh, huh, huh?"

Elizabeth frowned. "Not exactly," she admitted. In fact, Todd practically never called her. And when he did, the conversations were short. Like, *real* short. *Like, "Want to go to a movie next Friday? Yeah? Good. OK, bye,"* Elizabeth thought, wondering if maybe she'd been too quick to defend him.

"So he's taking you for granted," Jessica concluded.

Elizabeth turned to put the bag of chips onto the snack shelf. She suddenly saw Todd in her mind's eye. Todd laughing with his buddies in the cafeteria instead of sitting with her. Todd who almost never held her hand in the movies. Todd who never sent her flowers, never even picked a bunch of dandelions for her.

"And this is *Valentine's* Day," Jessica argued. "If he's not going to show you he cares on *Valentine's* Day, then—"

Elizabeth shoved the chips onto the shelf, but she didn't turn around. She bit her lip. Maybe there was something to what Jessica was saying after all.

She liked Todd. He was cute and fun to be with. And smart, and he had a great sense of humor.

But when it comes to the true romance department, Todd isn't anything to write home about, Elizabeth thought, wrinkling her nose.

"Oh, Steven!" Jessica said brightly. She had finished putting the groceries away (well, OK, Elizabeth had done most of the work) and was hanging out on the front porch of the house.

Steven scowled as he approached the door.

"Yeah? What do you want *this* time, Jessica?"

Jessica decided to ignore Steven's tone of voice. "Oh, I was just thinking," she said casually. "You know, about your basketball team."

"Uh-huh," Steven said sourly, pushing his way past her. "Hey, did you guys do the shopping? Did you pick up the four half gallons of strawberry ripple that I put on the list? A guy's gotta eat, you know."

Jessica moved quickly to block the door. "You know, um, Pete Claybaugh?" she asked, flashing him a sunny smile and resting a hand on his shoulder. "From the team, I mean."

"Sure I know Pete," Steven said, rolling his eyes. "He's a senior." He shook his head and swept his hair out of his eyes. "And he doesn't have a steady girlfriend," he said meaningfully, adding something under his breath that sounded like, "Lucky guy."

Jessica frowned, wondering why Steven seemed so down about having a steady girlfriend. But she had better things to worry about. "He's got a couple of really good-looking cousins," she said quickly. "How about arranging an introduction for us?"

Steven ran a hand through his hair. "'Us?'" he asked pointedly, staring from side to side. "Who's 'us'? You and the little green men hiding in the bushes?"

Jessica blushed. "Well, Elizabeth and me." *At least, Elizabeth and me after I talk her into it,* she corrected herself. *Which shouldn't be too hard—right?* "Anyway—"

Steven gestured impatiently. "A couple of girls move to town and you need *me* to—"

"Not *girls*," Jessica interrupted. "*Guys*. Not everyone cute is a girl, you know."

Steven snorted. "Could have fooled me," he said. Shaking off Jessica's grip, he marched through the door and yelled, "I'm home!"

Jessica licked her lips nervously. If Steven wouldn't cooperate, she'd have to figure out another way of meeting the brothers—and she wasn't sure how. "Listen, Steven," she begged, following her brother into the living room. "This is, like, important. See, there's this street dance coming up and—"

"I *know* about the street dance, OK?" Steven snapped. He kicked off his shoes and tumbled onto the couch.

"Oh. Yeah, of course," Jessica said quickly, hoping she hadn't offended her brother. *Of course he knows about it*, she reminded herself. High-school kids would be there too, and Joe Howell's garage band was scheduled to play. "Um—you'll be going with Cathy, right?"

"I guess so," Steven sighed from deep inside the couch.

Jessica wondered again why Steven sounded so down. Quickly she explained the situation, hoping her brother was actually bothering to listen. "So we were hoping that you'd talk to Pete and help us meet—," she was finishing up, when Elizabeth came into the room. She blushed. "I mean, *I* was hoping—"

"Get real." Steven swung his legs over the edge

of the couch and stood up suddenly, arms hanging loosely at his sides. "I'm not a message boy. Anyway, sixth-graders don't need dates for some stupid street dance."

"But—" Jessica protested. She hadn't expected Steven to be so snotty about it.

"But, nothing," Steven told her. "Right now, I'm getting a glass of milk. Then, I'm getting ready for my date. And *if* I talk to Pete Claybaugh this weekend, *which* I seriously doubt, I won't even *mention* his cousins. That OK with you? Good. It better be." With long strides, Steven walked toward the kitchen.

Jessica made a face and chewed a lock of her hair. *Now what?*

"Of all the nerve!" Elizabeth whispered. Jessica turned to see her twin standing in the middle of the room, hands on hips, staring angrily at Steven's back. "Some stupid street dance, huh?" She bit her lip. "We'll show him!"

Jessica managed a smile. That conversation with her brother had gotten one thing done anyway. It had made Elizabeth mad.

Which meant . . .

Slowly, Jessica's smile grew wider.

Maybe she could get her sister to listen to reason, after all.

Three

"So, do you think maybe you can talk to Steven?" Jessica asked Cathy hopefully.

Upstairs, Steven was still banging around in the bathroom. Cathy had showed up early for the date, and Jessica was using the extra time to tell Cathy about the Claybaugh brothers. "See, I couldn't convince him to talk to Pete, but maybe if you told him to. . . . " Her voice trailed off.

"You don't really *have* to," Elizabeth said, sounding embarrassed.

Jessica gave her sister a dig in the ribs. "Quiet!" she hissed. Getting Elizabeth just to agree to think about this had *not* been easy.

"Sure, I'll talk to him," Cathy promised. "Of course, I don't know if it'll do any good."

Jessica nodded slowly. "But you do think that

it's OK for sixth-graders to go to dances with dates—right?"

Cathy nodded. "A hundred percent," she agreed. "And I can understand why you're upset about Aaron."

Jessica smiled. She'd always liked Cathy. In fact, she thought Cathy was too good for her brother the jerk. *She's kind of the older sister I never had,* she said to herself. An older sister would talk to Pete for her, she was sure. Too bad Cathy didn't know Pete very well.

"What movie are you guys going to see tonight?" Elizabeth asked.

Cathy frowned. "I'm not really sure," she admitted. "But it's Friday night, and we always go to the movies together Friday night. Steven said he'd choose a good one."

"A good one?" Jessica wrinkled her nose. "He'll probably pick something dumb. Something like *Danger Zone, Part Six.*"

Cathy smiled. "Oh, I don't think he'd do that, Jessica," she said. "*Danger Zone* is something he might see with Joe Howell and his other buddies. But he knows that's not my kind of show." She shook her head. "The review in the paper said there were seventy-six dead bodies in the first hour alone."

"Really?" Jessica's eyes widened. "Seventy-six?"

"That's what the review said," Cathy confirmed. "Personally, I hope I never find out."

Jessica took a deep breath. She decided she didn't want to find out either.

*   *   *

"Hey, Cathy," Steven said, crossing the room and giving Cathy a quick kiss on the cheek. Elizabeth grinned. Showered and dressed in a clean T-shirt, her brother actually looked almost human for a change.

Cathy reached for his hand. "No flowers?" Her eyes twinkled.

"Flowers?" Steven made a face.

Cathy laughed. "Listen, Steven," she went on, "I've been talking to your sisters."

"Big mistake," Steven muttered.

Cathy bit her lip. "Why don't you just call your friend Pete and ask him to help your sisters out? It wouldn't be hard."

Steven rolled his eyes. "I don't know why I should do everything just because I'm the older brother."

Elizabeth wrinkled her nose. She still wasn't sure she liked Jessica's idea of asking the Claybaugh brothers to the dance, but she was disappointed that Steven wouldn't lift a finger to help. "It's not because you're the older brother," she said. "It's because you're the one who knows their cousin."

Steven's only response was a short barking laugh.

Cathy shrugged at the twins. "I'll try again," she promised in a whisper. "What movie did you want to see?" she asked Steven, flashing him a bright smile.

"*Danger Zone, Part Six,*" Steven said sharply. Dropping Cathy's hand, he took her elbow and started toward the door. "And we're going to be late, so we'd better hurry."

"*Danger Zone?*" Cathy frowned. "But, Steven, you know that's not my kind of movie."

"You'll like it," Steven said impatiently. "You shouldn't be prejudiced against movies you've never seen, just because there's a bunch of dead bodies and a couple of explosions and one scene where a guy gets his head chopped off by a helicopter. Being prejudiced isn't, like, a good character trait." He turned to face Cathy. "Anyway, *Danger Zone*'s what I'm seeing tonight. You coming or not?"

Cathy bit her lip. "Um—I'm coming," she said.

"Good." Steven's face relaxed into a grin. Together he and Cathy walked out. The door banged behind them.

"It just goes to show you," Jessica remarked, hands on hips. "You can give a jerk a shower and put him into a clean T-shirt. But it doesn't change his essential jerkiness."

Elizabeth shook her head. Outside the house she could hear Cathy and Steven talking, their voices drifting down the quiet sidewalk and in through the window screens.

"But, Steven—" Cathy protested.

Steven snorted. "Hey, I should get to do stuff I want to do once in a while, OK?"

Elizabeth took a deep breath. Steven suddenly

reminded her uncomfortably of somebody else she knew. Somebody who didn't always think about her needs. Somebody who didn't write little notes or send bouquets or—

"And you know what the worst of it is, Lizzie?" Jessica hissed. "After a couple of years of steady dating with Todd, you know what he's going to be like?" She paused dramatically and pointed out the door. "Just exactly like—"

But Elizabeth didn't need her sister to finish the sentence. She'd already made the connection. *Todd Wilkins plus a couple of years equals—*

She shuddered. *Equals Steven Wakefield.*

"So you'd better be in on this Claybaugh brothers thing," Jessica went on. "Because if you aren't, Todd's just going to go on taking you for granted and getting worse and worse and—"

Elizabeth sighed. "Save your breath, Jess!" she told her twin. After watching the way Steven had treated Cathy tonight, maybe she *was* ready to show Todd that he wasn't the only guy in the world. "Count me in!"

"But the movie doesn't start for fifteen minutes," Cathy said. "Why did we rush?"

Steven grabbed a huge handful of popcorn and stuffed it into his mouth. He rested his long legs on the back of the seat in front of him and stared fixedly at the empty screen. He wished Cathy would just shut up already. "Because," he said through the popcorn, not bothering to offer the tub to Cathy. "Because I wanted to make sure we got good seats, OK?"

"But—" Cathy looked around the mostly empty theater, frowning. "There are plenty of good seats, Steven. Why didn't—"

"Because!" Steven snapped. *No, scratch that*, he told himself. He hadn't meant to sound like a jerk. *If there's one thing I'm not*, he thought, *it's a jerk.* He took a deep breath. "Listen, Cathy," he said in a more friendly tone, "it's not that I'm mad at you or anything. It's just that—" He paused.

Cathy turned to face him. "Just that what?" she asked.

Steven stared directly into her eyes for a second. Then he dropped his gaze and filled his mouth with popcorn again. "Oh, I don't know," he said dismissively. "It's not you, though, OK?"

"OK." Cathy frowned. "But I wish you'd be more—"

"I said it's not you!" Steven barked, wishing they'd start the stupid movie so he wouldn't have to talk to Cathy anymore. He didn't want to hurt her. He still liked her an awful lot. Admired her too. But Joe's words were ringing in his ear. All the stuff he'd said about not being tied down. About getting bored. *This is, what, the sixty-third Friday night in a row that we've spent together?*

"But, Steven—" Cathy tried again. She stroked the back of his hand and leaned closer.

Steven bit his lip and pulled his hand away. He just wasn't in the mood for it right now. "Like I *said*, Cathy—"

"All right, all right!" Cathy pulled her own hand back. She set her jaw and stared forward at the blank screen too.

What a pair, Steven thought, tossing more popcorn into his mouth. *Together, but apart.* "Want some popcorn?" he asked grudgingly, handing her the tub.

Cathy didn't turn to look at him. She gave a slight shake of the head.

"OK, OK," Steven said, glad that she hadn't said yes. *More for me. And you can't say I didn't try.* He munched another mouthful. The thought began to occur to him that maybe Joe had been wrong. Maybe Steven Wakefield wasn't really a one-woman kind of guy at all.

Steven nodded to himself. Yeah. It wasn't Cathy's problem or anything; she was truly cool, and it was just eating him up that he couldn't treat her nicely. But maybe it was like gluing wings on a fish and asking it to fly. *I'm too young to be tied down, that's the deal,* he told himself. It sounded pretty good, so he thought it again. *I'm too young to be tied down yet, and if I keep going out with Cathy every stupid Friday night I'll hurt her eventually, even though it's, like, the last thing in the world I'd do on purpose.*

With a sigh he looked around the theater. It was beginning to fill up. His pulse quickened as he saw a familiar group of guys come in and sit a few rows ahead of him. All the cool guys at school. He recognized Richard Ferris, the captain of the basketball team, and a few others he knew slightly. The Big Men on Campus, they called themselves.

That's where I belong, he thought. *With the guys. Only—*

How can I be with the guys when I'm with Cathy all the time?

He glanced over at Cathy, who was still watching the empty screen. Steven sighed. Much as he liked her, he wished they had a—well, a different kind of relationship. The kind where he could call her whenever he wanted to see her, but there'd be none of this every-Friday-night nonsense just because they were a couple. He should be able to cancel any time, for any reason, without her getting mad. He nodded. *Yup. That's the way to go—*

"Hey, Wakefield!"

Startled, Steven looked up from the popcorn. Ferris was waving at him! He was being recognized by one of the truly cool dudes at Sweet Valley High. Hesitating only for a second, he vaulted out of his seat, brushed past Cathy, and headed down the aisle to where Ferris was sitting. "Hey, Ferris, how you doing?" he asked, trying hard to act cool.

Ferris shrugged. "Not bad, man. How's life?" He didn't wait for an answer. Instead, he put an empty popcorn tub onto the head of Matt Johnston, the freshman who was sitting next to him. With a thump, he whacked the tub so it fit neatly over Johnston's ears.

"Hey!" Johnston protested.

Ferris laughed. It *was* kind of funny, Steven decided, so he joined in, grateful it hadn't happened to him.

Ferris winked at Steven. "Nice hat," he said to Johnston. "You could probably get a date now, know what I mean?"

"Sure improves your looks," Kevin McAndrew jeered.

"I get plenty of dates!" Johnston pulled off the tub and kicked it down a few rows. "More than you get, Ferris."

"In your dreams," Ferris said calmly.

Steven admired how cool and collected Ferris was, how much he was in control of everything. He wished he could be like that.

"I get a date any time I want," Ferris went on, smiling broadly. "No reason to be tied down, huh, Wakefield? Not with so many hot girls out there to choose from."

"N-no," Steven agreed. *First Joe, now Ferris*, he thought. It seemed like nobody was going steady anymore. Nobody but him.

"Aren't you here with Connors?" Ferris asked lazily.

"With, um, Cathy, you mean?" Steven fumbled for words. "Um, well, yeah. I mean, no. Sort of. We're not really *with* each other," he lied, the words coming more easily now. "We're just, you know, friends. Just, like, sitting next to each other, is all," he finished, wondering why his palms were suddenly so sweaty. *Must be the popcorn oil*, he decided.

"Oh." Ferris clearly wasn't interested. The house lights began to darken.

"About time!" Patrick shouted.

"Woo, woo, woo!" McAndrew yelled out. "Dead-body city, here we come!"

"Seen this movie before?" Ferris asked. "It's incredibly awesome, man. I've seen it, like, eight times. I think a hundred and twelve people get it, live and on-screen. In full color."

A hundred and twelve? Steven frowned. He had nothing against dead bodies, but a hundred and twelve did seem a little much.

"Have a seat if you want," Ferris offered, resting his arm against the back of his chair and pointing down the row. "We don't bite. Not even *Patrick* bites."

Frank Patrick grimaced and showed his teeth.

"Oh. Um, thanks." Steven's head spun. The first promo began on the screen above his head. He stole a quick look back at Cathy. It was quite an honor to be asked to sit with the Big Men. As long as they didn't put a popcorn bucket over his head or anything.

And then there was Cathy. He really should consider her feelings.

But if he couldn't treat her nicely . . . and if the coolest guys at school were asking him to sit with them . . .

Steven stood frozen over Ferris's seat, wondering what on earth he should do.

*   *   *

"Then it's settled," Jessica said, her eyes sparkling. "At about nine o'clock, we'll just kind of casually walk by Pete's house. Maybe we'll, you know, bump into them."

Elizabeth nodded. The cousins could be outside, even at nine. "They'll be skateboarding or something," she guessed.

"Yeah." Jessica's grin grew wider. "Maybe I could, like, fall down when they come by and pretend to be hurt big time. You know, like one of them ran me over with his skateboard? Then they'd have to take us inside and put bandages on me and—"

"Whoa!" Elizabeth cut in. *Trust Jessica to come up with some crazy scheme.* She shook her head. "You can't do that."

Jessica made a face. "You're right," she admitted.

"Good," Elizabeth said. "So we'll just walk around and—"

"I mean, *I* can't do it," Jessica interrupted. "I couldn't be convincing, because I'm so graceful they'd *know* I'd get out of the way. But you!" She clapped Elizabeth on the back. "*You* could do it! You're, like, a total klutz anyway!"

Elizabeth frowned. "What do you mean, I'm—"

Jessica tugged at her sister's arm. "Come on, let's hear your fake screams!"

"So, you sitting or not?" Ferris demanded.

Steven's mouth felt dry. "Um—" he began.

"That is—" He was careful not to look at Cathy. "I just, really—" *For crying out loud, what am I trying to say anyway?*

Ferris groaned loudly. "Look, kid, this isn't, like, an IQ test. Sit, or don't sit, who cares?"

Steven glanced in anguish back toward Cathy. As much as he wanted to leave her for the Big Men, he couldn't let her stay there all alone.

Wait a minute.

Cathy wasn't alone after all. He held his breath. *Yes!* A couple of her friends had come into the theater and were sitting on either side of her. Well, *that* made things easy. He wouldn't really be abandoning her now, right? And the way things were, she'd probably enjoy their company more than his anyway.

But still, a little voice in his head told him, *if you brought her you really ought to sit with her.*

Steven squeezed his eyes shut and shook his head, hoping to shut that little voice up. When he opened his eyes again, he was facing the row directly behind Ferris's—where, sitting all by herself, was Jill Hale. The girl he'd had the hots for before Cathy came along.

His heart gave a leap. Jill was just as beautiful as he'd remembered her being. No. More. The scent she used to wear came suddenly into his nostrils. He shut his eyes again, remembering how he used to feel about Jill, remembering how hard he'd tried to get to know her, remembering how happy he'd been when she'd agreed to go out with him that one time.

He breathed deeply. He could feel the same way about her again, he was sure.

And after going out with Cathy for so long, maybe he needed just a little change. Nothing against Cathy, of course. Just that he needed a little oomph. A little extra. A little Jill Hale.

Jill's eyes flicked away from the screen. He gripped the back of Ferris's chair tightly. He could hardly breathe—Jill was looking directly at him, smiling, he could have sworn it!

And if he moved all the way down to the end of Ferris's row, he'd be right in front of Jill. Steven's mouth was drier than ever. His palms wouldn't quit sweating. He knew he probably should be getting back to Cathy, but how could he turn away from Jill?

Almost without knowing what he was doing, he began climbing over legs to the end of the row.

Four

"Cool movie, man. Way cool," Kevin McAndrew said. He stood up and stretched.

"Yeah," Steven agreed, stretching too. The movie had been pretty awesome, all right. Well, maybe the scene with the helicopter had been a little bit gruesome. But Ferris and his buddies seemed to think it was a riot. Things didn't seem quite so disgusting with a laugh track, somehow. "How many times have you seen it?"

"Twelve," McAndrew told him. "You?" he asked, but he didn't sound as if he cared about the answer.

"Three times," Steven lied. "You sure know it real well," he added. McAndrew had shouted out practically every line of dialogue along with the actors.

Not that there had been very many lines of dialogue.

"Yeah." McAndrew shrugged and turned to the other end of the row. "Hey, Ferris, what'd you think?" he called.

"Awesome, as usual," Ferris said with a grin.

"Pretty cool, huh?" Steven said, trying to catch Ferris's eye, but Ferris didn't respond. Steven sighed. Maybe he ought to go check on Cathy, he thought with a twinge of guilt, trying not to think about Jill in the row behind him. He had been acutely aware of her throughout the entire movie. *But I came with Cathy, and I ought to leave with Cathy,* he told himself nobly. *No matter what. Steven the Martyr, that's me.*

He turned and squinted in the bright lights for his date. But the seat where he'd left her a hundred and twelve dead bodies ago was empty.

Frowning, Steven looked left and right. Maybe she'd changed seats? He hoped she'd liked the movie, and in a way he wasn't sorry he'd brought her. Open her mind a little bit. Give her new experiences, and all that.

Still no Cathy. Steven turned directly around. A familiar scent met his nostrils, and he stood stock-still.

"Hi there, Steven," Jill Hale said in a husky voice.

"I'm telling you, these guys are *foxes*," Jessica said in a half whisper. "Babes, both of them." She knelt against the hedge that surrounded the Claybaughs' house. "Of course, I think you'd prefer the younger one. He's more your type."

Elizabeth knew that was code for "Keep your hands off the older one." "It's getting late," she whispered back. "Don't you think we'd better just go home?"

"Go home?" Jessica's eyes blazed. "And let Janet and Kimberly and Lila get their claws into these guys?"

"It's already past nine-thirty," Elizabeth pointed out. "We've been here for over half an hour, and we haven't seen a sign of them." They'd walked back and forth in front of the house six times at least, but no luck. They'd even tried to sneak a peek in through a window to see if the boys were home— *well, Jessica did anyway,* Elizabeth assured herself, glad that she hadn't been a part of that one—but the window only looked into a pantry, and the pantry door was shut. "And it's cold and—"

"Don't you wimp out on me now," Jessica said, narrowing her eyes and staring hard at her twin. "It's, like, *death* for me if one of my friends winds up with one of these guys."

For about the millionth time Elizabeth wondered how Jessica defined the word "friend." The Unicorns were more competitive with each other than anyone she'd ever met. "But you don't even know the boys' *names,*" she pointed out.

"Details." Jessica waved her hand grandly. "Anyway," she added, her eyes growing dark, "if you leave me now I'll—wait." She drew in her breath. "Did you hear that?" she whispered.

"What?" Elizabeth asked, but then she heard it too. There was a sudden rustling of leaves, and a voice came out of the bushes behind them.

"What are you two doing?" it hissed.

"How've you been?" Jill purred, batting her eyelashes.

"Um—fine." Steven felt weak in the knees. He breathed deeply, remembering the incredible crush he'd had on Jill way back when. "How are you?" he asked, trying to keep his voice steady. She was even hotter than he remembered. Next to her, Cathy seemed—well, she just didn't have the same radiance, the same glow, the same . . . Steven tried hard to think of the exact word.

"Oh, fine," Jill said with a laugh.

Like the peal of a bell, Steven thought, proud to remember that image from a poem he'd read in English class.

"I'm surprised to see you here," Jill cooed. "I didn't know you were friends with Richard and his crowd. You've come such a long way." She smiled, showing teeth as white and even as—as—

"Oh, yeah," Steven mumbled, feeling his cheeks turn red. "Did you, you know, like the movie?"

Jill smiled again.

As white and even as a whole lot of sugar cubes, Steven decided, staring at her perfect teeth. *Or maybe pearls. Of course, pearls.*

"You bet," Jill replied. "Like, the color was so cool! And the acting was very sophisticated."

"It was?" Steven raised his eyebrows. *Sophisticated* wasn't the word he would have used to describe it. But he didn't want to argue with Jill. "Oh, sure. I mean, like, *really* sophisticated." He watched as she reached up to pat her hair, which shimmered like—like a flash of lightning. Once again, his palms felt clammy, and he knew it wasn't just from the popcorn.

"I'm so glad you agree!" Jill trilled, leaning a touch closer to Steven and staring him right in the eye.

Steven took a deep breath. *She's going for me!* he thought with delight. Then, in the next moment, he was sure she wasn't. Hadn't she been dating Ferris? No, couldn't be. Ferris had just been talking about how great it was to play the field. Maybe he dumped her? Or she dumped him?

No. Steven frowned, concentrating on Jill's beautiful eyes, which floated in front of him like liquid pools of—oh, never mind. No way Jill had dumped Ferris; he'd sounded too happy about being out on his own.

"Are you, um, dating anybody right now, Steven?" Jill asked, moving closer still.

Steven gulped. "Um—well," he stammered. *Relax. She's just curious*, he assured himself. "That is—" He hesitated. But what if Jill wasn't just curious? *What if she's, you know, interested?* "I mean—"

A hand clapped his shoulder. "Hey, Wakefield.

Coming for pizza?" Ferris demanded. He didn't seem to notice Jill.

"Pizza," Steven repeated. "Yeah. I mean—"

Jill yawned and stared off into the distance with a look of total boredom.

Now what? Steven thought miserably. It was an awful choice. *Torn between friends who aren't really your friends yet and a girl who ought to be your girlfriend only she doesn't know it yet either—*

"Make up your mind, buddy. We don't have all night." Ferris's grip tightened.

I'll invite her to come along, Steven thought. *No. On second thought—* He could just see Ferris making a play for her.

"Well, if you're going to be doing dumb *boy* stuff—" Jill said with a sniff.

Steven took a deep breath. That was a hint, wasn't it? He turned to Ferris. "Thanks," he said, "but Jill and I are going skating. Right, Jill?" He let the air out with a whoosh. "We sure are," Jill said, turning back to Steven with a big smile and leaning against his side.

Ferris stared from Steven to Jill. Then he shrugged. "Have it your way," he said. "See you around, Wakefield," he added meaningfully.

Steven could feel his heart racing. He'd done it. He'd kind of asked Jill out. And in front of all the coolest guys in school, including the captain of his very own basketball team. He considered raising his fists in the air like a heavyweight boxer celebrating a victory in the ring, but he felt too weak. And hungry. "So we'll skate," he said, turning to Jill, "but we could, like, grab a burger before. If you wanted."

"Are you sure you're not, you know, dating anybody?" Jill asked, a worried expression on her face. "I thought I'd been seeing you around with Cathy Connors."

She spoke the name as if it were a disease, but Steven was too pleased with himself to care. "Well," he admitted, scuffing the carpet with the tip of his shoe, "sort of. Off and on." He shrugged casually. "Nothing serious." His stomach churned at the lie. But to win over Jill, anything was fair. *Right?* "So, what do you think? About the burger, I mean."

Jill raised her head and smiled. "Sure, Steven!" she said, sounding pleased. "I'd love to."

Steven put his hand on Jill's elbow, basking in what he was certain were admiring stares. Slowly, he led her out the exit, thrilled and nervous at the same time.

"Don't lose your lunch!" Cathy Connors said. "It's only me."

Elizabeth's heart was thundering in her chest. She leaned against the bushes, breathing hard. "You scared us!" she said, looking around for her brother. "And where's Steven?"

Cathy made a face. "Sorry for scaring you," she said, kicking a pebble. "As for Steven, I don't know where he is. And at the moment I'm not sure I care either."

This sounded serious. "What happened?" Elizabeth asked.

"Oh, nothing," Cathy said grimly. "He just kind of abandoned me at the theater, that's all. He went to sit with some of his really cool friends."

"Cool friends?" Jessica burst out. "Was Pete Claybaugh one of them?"

Elizabeth nudged Jessica, trying to focus on Cathy. "He just left you all by yourself?"

"It's like I said," Jessica muttered. "You can't take away his basic jerkiness. Steven minus all the jerkiness equals zero."

Cathy considered. "Well," she admitted. "I guess it wasn't quite that bad. We'd kind of had an argument. And he did leave me sitting with some of my friends." She smiled faintly. "Actually, the movie was so repulsive, we left after twenty minutes and went to watch the rest of the new Eileen Thomas film instead."

"Good for you," Elizabeth said approvingly. Eileen Thomas was one of her favorite movie actresses.

"Anyway, that's the sad story," Cathy went on. "Right now I'm on my way home to grab my skates. Then I'll be meeting my friends at the skating rink." She sighed. "Like they say, if life hands you a lemon, make lemonade."

Elizabeth shook her head sadly. She knew exactly which lemon Cathy was talking about.

Cathy frowned. "Oh, this is Pete Claybaugh's house, isn't it?"

"We're stalking them," Jessica explained. "Like I keep telling my sister, there is no way on earth I am showing my face at the dance without a date. No way at all."

"Well, I don't know," Elizabeth said wearily. "If Steven treats Cathy this way, how do we know these brothers would treat us any better?"

Jessica snorted. "They'll treat us better," she predicted. "I can feel it in my bones. Just by looking at them, I can tell." She peered around the bushes. "Trust me, Elizabeth."

Elizabeth bit her lip. She looked at Cathy for help.

But Cathy shook her head. "She's right, Elizabeth," she said. "This happened because Steven only thought about himself. He took me for granted. And it could happen to you too," she went on gravely, looking Elizabeth in the eye. "What's the name of that boy you kind of like?"

"Todd," Elizabeth said. "But Todd wouldn't just leave me the way Steven left you. Not Todd. And anyway, it's just a basketball game." The colder she got, the more she was willing to give Todd the benefit of the doubt.

Cathy looked sad. "You know, Elizabeth, when I first started dating Steven, that's what I said to myself. 'Not Steven.' No way would Steven think about his own needs and ignore mine. That's what I *said*," she repeated, eyes scanning Elizabeth's face. "But it happens. As tonight just proved."

"Well, yeah, but—" Elizabeth's voice trailed off. Cammi Adams's face flashed into her mind. She wrinkled her nose. She liked Cammi and all that, and she didn't really think Todd would leave her and go off somewhere with Cammi instead. Still . . .

"Even Todd could abandon you at the movies, you know," Cathy said. She checked her watch. "Well. I'd better go. Good luck, you two. Hope you do better than I did tonight!"

Even Todd. Elizabeth watched Cathy go. Could Todd actually abandon her in the movies? Probably not.

She bit her lip. *Probably* not.

"Well?" Jessica barked. "You staying or going?"

Elizabeth sighed. "Staying, I guess," she grumbled as she knelt down by the bushes again. "But only for another half hour."

Five

"What are you two doing—playing detective?"

Jessica swung around, recognizing the sarcastic voice right away. It belonged to Janet Howell, the president of the Unicorn Club and the last person Jessica wanted to see at that moment.

"Um, hi, Janet," she said, smiling weakly at her friend. Her mind raced. She couldn't possibly tell Janet what she was really up to. Janet was sort of moonstruck over Denny Jacobson, but Jessica suspected that Denny was going to the Glenwood game, just like Aaron. Which meant that Janet was in the market for a date to the street dance too. Which meant—

"Well, you see, Janet," Elizabeth began, straightening up, "Pete Claybaugh has—"

Jessica brought her heel down on Elizabeth's

foot. "Oh, sorry, I tripped!" she announced loudly, pushing her sister onto her knees for good measure. "Hey, Janet," she added as she helped Elizabeth up, "we just saw Denny walking by."

"We did?" Elizabeth looked confused.

"Yeah," Jessica said, staring daggers at her twin. "He was heading down toward the Dairi Burger, I think." She crossed her fingers behind her back. "And I *think* he was with some other girl," she went on. *There. That ought to do it.*

Janet stepped back, a frown on her face. "*Denny?*"

Jessica shrugged. "It was hard to tell. You know, it was already dark and everything. But it sure looked like him."

Janet took a deep breath. "It wasn't Ellen he was with, was it? I just bet it was," she murmured, looking murderously down the street. "The way she's been talking to him the last few days—"

"Ellen?" Jessica scratched her ear, trying to look virtuous. It was a shame to get her friend Ellen Riteman in trouble with the Unicorn president, but it was even more important to get rid of Janet. She stole a quick glance at the Claybaughs' front door, hoping that the brothers wouldn't burst out of the house just now. "It *might* have been Ellen. But it was hard to tell."

"I'm going to kill her," Janet said simply, her eyes glinting in the darkness. "To the Dairi Burger, you said?" She whirled and stared down the block.

"Just wait till I catch up with them. Thanks for the info, Jessica." She strode off down the sidewalk.

Jessica heaved a sigh of relief. She'd done it. Their secret was safe—for now.

"You're something else," Elizabeth said, shaking her head. "Janet's going to be mad at Denny, and she'll probably try to kick Ellen out of the Unicorns. All because of a couple of boys you don't even know." She sighed.

"Yeah, well," Jessica snapped. To tell the truth, she did feel a twinge of guilt. But only a tiny one. "They'll work it out," she went on. "And if Denny and Janet decide to be mad at each other, that's *their* problem, not mine."

Elizabeth shook her head. "But they're supposed to be your *friends*, Jess."

Jessica opened her mouth for an angry retort, but she closed it abruptly.

The Claybaughs' front door was opening.

"Beautiful evening," Mrs. Claybaugh said, stretching and taking a deep breath of night air.

"It sure is." Pete's dad came onto the porch behind her. Elizabeth strained to see through the darkness. Were the brothers coming out? She couldn't see them anywhere. "Where are the guys?" she mouthed, turning to her sister.

"Wait," Jessica hissed confidently.

Mrs. Claybaugh looked up at the sky. "When are the kids getting back?"

Mr. Claybaugh sat down on the porch glider and rocked gently back and forth. "Any minute now," he told her. "Pete was taking them down to the beach for volleyball. Then he said he'd stop by the Dairi Burger on the way home and buy them dessert."

The Dairi Burger? Elizabeth's heart lurched.

Beside her she could hear Jessica's sharp intake of breath. "We've just sent the enemy right to them!" She stood up, twigs crackling. "Come on, let's roll."

On the porch, Mrs. Claybaugh turned toward the twins, a worried expression on her face. "What was that scratching noise?" she asked.

"Probably just squirrels," Mr. Claybaugh told her. He patted the seat next to him. "I'm so proud of Pete, showing his cousins around the way he is. I was guessing he'd just ignore them."

Jessica jerked hard on Elizabeth's hand. In an instant they were out of the bushes and heading toward the Dairi Burger.

"This is a *shortcut?*" Elizabeth panted. She stepped ankle-deep into a puddle and shuddered. "I don't know why we're going this way, Jessica. I can hardly see anything!"

Jessica hesitated, wondering whether to go straight or climb the Evanses' fence. "Of course it's a shortcut," she snapped. "I've been this way a zillion times."

"In the dark?" Elizabeth sounded doubtful.

"Sure, in the dark," Jessica lied. The fence way would be fastest, she decided. "Listen," she said as she hoisted herself up the links of chain, "we've got to get to the Dairi Burger before Janet does. If we don't—" She could just see it now, Janet calling her early tomorrow morning and saying in a smarmy voice, "Hi, Jessica. Guess who I met last night? Hey, you don't have a date for the street dance, do you?" Jessica took a deep breath and reached low to help her sister up. "If we don't," she said with feeling, "I'm *meat*."

"But—" Elizabeth frowned.

A dog barked. Jessica's blood froze. In a neighboring yard, a huge pit bull was throwing itself against a fence. *It can't get you*, she told herself. *The fence is in the way. . . .*

The dog lunged again, barking violently and rattling the metal. Jessica's mouth felt dry. The dog looked plenty big enough to knock the fence over. And then—

A woman's voice rang through the night. "Wimpy! Sleepy time, dear. Stop rattling the fence. Everything's all right."

Wimpy. Jessica breathed deeply. The dog didn't look wimpy at all. *It can't get me*, she told herself again, edging slowly forward. *And if I don't hurry, I'll miss Janet, and then—*

The dog lunged once more. A deep growl rumbled from its throat. Its eyes flashed. Jessica thought she saw sharp fangs.

"Wimpy!" The woman sounded firm. "Quiet,

babykins, or no doggie treat for breakfast!"

That did it. Slowly, the dog backed up and lay down, one ear almost covering its left eye. "Go!" Jessica hissed. In three strides, it seemed, she was across the Evanses' lawn and onto the sidewalk. The Dairi Burger was just down the block, and coming down the sidewalk toward them was—Janet.

"Jessica?" Janet looked surprised. "Didn't I just—"

"Oh, Janet!" Jessica put on the most frantic expression she could imagine. "Oh, Janet, it's really awful!"

"What is?" Janet stopped in her tracks and looked searchingly at Jessica.

"Yeah, what is?" Elizabeth murmured under her breath.

Jessica knew she was going to have to wing it. Somehow, she'd have to keep Janet out of the Dairi Burger. What could she say? Vicious dogs in the bathrooms? Puddles all over the floor? Poisoned doggy treats—*yes!* "It's the hamburgers, Janet," she explained, making her eyes wide with alarm. "It just came over the radio! The, um, health department announced that they found, like, dog hair in the Dairi Burgers!" No, dog hair wasn't gross enough. "I mean, roaches!" She elbowed her sister. "Right, Lizzie?"

"Roaches?" Janet turned pale. She put her hand to her mouth, and for a second Jessica thought she was going to barf right there on the sidewalk. "That's, like, totally scuzzy!"

Jessica nodded. Taking Janet by the arm, she turned her around. "So of *course* you don't want to go in there," she said. "You should go right home so you can—" *Throw up in your very own toilet*, she finished in her head, but she didn't dare say it out loud. Come to think of it, Janet really did look sick. Jessica stepped back, just in case.

But instead of heading back down the block, Janet broke into a run—straight toward the door of the Dairi Burger. "Where are you going?" Jessica gasped. "You *want* a belly full of roaches?"

"It's Denny!" Janet explained. "He loves Dairi Burgers, he's probably eating three of them right now, and if he eats a roach I'll never forgive myself!" She reached for the door.

Jessica thought hard. It seemed as if thinking hard was all she had been doing lately. "We'll go with you," she said quickly, grabbing the door before it could close after her friend.

After all, she thought grimly, *what choice do I have?*

"Denny?" Janet called. "Denny?" She blinked in the bright lights of the restaurant.

Elizabeth sighed. It seemed as if sighing was all she had been doing lately. "Jessica—" she began. In front of her she could see teenagers everywhere, munching on roach-free burgers with roach-free fries and roach-free cole slaw on the side. "Hasn't this gone far enough?"

"Are you out of your *mind?*" Jessica snarled. "Janet!" she called. "Janet, come here! I need to talk to you!"

"Denny?" Janet paid no attention. Her eyes were large and frightened. "Denny, stop eating! There are—"

Elizabeth's heart sank. *First Jessica skulks around and lies to her friends,* she thought. *And if that's not bad enough, now she's spreading rumors about one of the most popular hangouts in Sweet Valley!* All to go out with some guy she'd never even met.

"Do you hear me, Denny?" There was panic in Janet's voice. "They just said it on the radio, Denny! There are bugs in—"

Elizabeth hoped there was no one in the restaurant that she knew. *Good thing our dad's a lawyer,* she thought uncomfortably. She had a feeling they might need his services pretty soon. "Jessica!" she hissed. "Let's just leave."

"And miss out on *that?*" Jessica hissed, stabbing a forefinger toward a booth in the corner.

On *that?* Elizabeth blinked. Pete Claybaugh was sitting with his back to the girls. And on the other side of the table were—

Elizabeth gulped. *Jessica wasn't wrong,* she admitted to herself. The two guys facing Pete were two of the best-looking kids she'd seen in, like, forever. They had perfect skin and teeth. The older one had dark curly hair and an impish grin that made Elizabeth understand why her sister thought he was so cute. As for the other—well, Elizabeth could only stare. Blond and dark-eyed, with an athletic build, a sincere smile that just wouldn't quit, and—

"See what I mean?" Jessica hissed. "Quick, block 'em so she doesn't see." She darted after Janet.

Feeling foolish, Elizabeth hustled toward the Claybaughs' table. "My, what interesting paint!" she exclaimed, bending to stroke the woodwork and making sure she was directly between the boys and Janet.

"Hey, these sundaes are pretty decent," one of the brothers said. Elizabeth didn't dare turn around to see which, but she was pretty certain it was the younger one. *Even his voice is nice,* she thought with a grin.

"Denny?" Janet turned and stared directly at Elizabeth. No. Directly *past* Elizabeth. Suddenly Elizabeth's mouth felt dry as a bone. "Den-ny!"

"Don't look, Janet!" Jessica clasped her hands firmly around Janet's eyes from behind. "Ugh, disgusto! A roach just crawled out of that girl's salad!"

With a scream, Janet pulled loose. Darting forward, she scanned the tables. "Denny? Denny? Has anybody seen Denny Jacobson? Tall, blond, good-looking?"

"Elizabeth!" Jessica mouthed over Janet's shoulder.

Elizabeth straightened up and stretched out her arms so Janet couldn't get past. "Ho hum, I'm exhausted!" she said, leaning back in case Janet tried to squeeze through. For good measure she threw in a yawn. "I don't know why I'm so tired." *Pretty idiotic, Elizabeth,* she thought with disgust. But it was the best measure she could come up with on short notice.

"Denny!" Janet threw herself toward Elizabeth. Craning her neck, she peered over Elizabeth's head and into the booth where the Claybaughs were sitting.

"Oh, Janet!" Jessica pulled Janet back, just in the nick of time. "I saw Denny! He's, like, in the bathroom!"

"In the bathroom?" Janet turned and ran.

Jessica followed, narrowly missing a little boy blowing straw wrappers into the air, and threw open the door to the ladies' room. "In here!" she commanded.

Janet pulled to a stop. "In the ladies' room?" she asked, but she ran in anyway.

"Whatever." Jessica slammed the door shut and winked triumphantly at Elizabeth. "You hold her in here," she hissed to her twin, "while I—" She broke off suddenly and raised her right arm. "Oops," she said innocently. "I think the door somehow got locked from the outside."

"It did?" Elizabeth leaned over to see.

"Yup," Jessica said, smiling brightly. "I just touched that little button there and presto!" She snapped her fingers.

"Denny?" Janet asked from inside, her voice catching. "Are—are you there?"

"We'll call the manager, Janet, don't worry," Jessica said, a wolfish grin on her face.

"Let me out!" From inside the bathroom came the rattling noise of a knob turning around and around, but the door didn't budge. "Jessica!"

Elizabeth allowed herself a small smile. The whole thing *was* kind of funny, she had to admit. She turned to check on the brothers, torn between insisting that Janet be let out right away and wanting to talk to the boys first instead.

But the boys weren't there.

The booth was empty. The remains of three ice cream sundaes sat on the table, along with a bunch of crumpled paper napkins and some coins for a tip.

The Claybaughs were gone.

"Which way did they go?" Jessica demanded, throwing open the front door of the Dairi Burger and staring into the parking lot.

"I don't know," Elizabeth admitted.

Jessica gritted her teeth. *So close to nabbing them—and yet so far. If it hadn't been for that stupid Janet Howell.*

She saw a flash of red. A car was pulling out. "Is that them?" she asked, grabbing her sister's arm and yanking her down the stairs toward the moving car.

"Um—" Elizabeth frowned. "I don't know."

"Well, find out!" Jessica snapped. "Go lie down in front of it or something!" She couldn't bear to lose the cousins again. And if Janet ever got out of the bathroom and found out what was going on— well, she'd never hear the end of it. "I *said*—"

"Wait a minute." Elizabeth stared past the car

and pointed. "Do you see what I see?" she asked, a note of horror in her voice.

Jessica groaned. "This is no time for guessing games, Elizabeth! This is life and death. This is—" She stopped abruptly as she realized what her sister was pointing at. "Oh, man," she breathed. "This is unbelievable."

She swallowed hard. But there was no mistake.

Coming down the sidewalk, holding hands as if they'd been dating for years, were Steven Wakefield—and Jill Hale.

"Completely revolting," Elizabeth muttered, her mouth tightening. Her heart ached for Cathy. Poor, poor Cathy.

Or maybe, poor Jill. Did she know what she was getting herself into?

A horn honked. In the dim light, Elizabeth could just make out Pete Claybaugh at the wheel of the car pulling out of the lot. At his side was the really cute cousin. Elizabeth's heart thudded. "Hey, Wakefield!" Pete called out, sticking his hand out the window in greeting.

"Hey, Claybaugh!" Steven slapped Pete five as the car turtled past. He preened and wound his other arm around Jill's waist. "Nice set of wheels, man! They new?"

"Barf city," Jessica grumbled, pointing into her throat.

Pete laughed easily. "Nice girlfriend, man. She

new?" He gunned the engine. The car leapt forward. "See you around, buddy."

"You know Pete?" Jill asked in a little baby-doll voice.

Steven laughed casually. "Oh, sure. Me and Pete go *way* back." He flashed Jill a wide smile and brushed his hair out of his eyes with an oh-so-casual gesture.

"Oh, *please*," Jessica groaned.

Elizabeth bit her lip. Steven was reminding her of a little kid who'd found a frog and had to show it off to everyone he knew. Or a cat who'd caught a bird and—

"After you, ma'am," Steven said gallantly, bending into an extravagant bow.

Jill tittered. "Oh, Steven, you do say the cleverest things!"

"Yeah, well," Steven said modestly, hurrying toward the door. "Here, let me get that for you. Ladies first!"

Elizabeth rolled her eyes and moved back into the shadows.

One thing was for sure. She had never been so nauseated in her entire life.

The Dairi Burger was a little more chaotic than usual, Steven thought as he found a table by the phone booth and helped Jill into her seat. In the background he could make out some manager type wiggling the door to the ladies' room with a fork while somebody inside was yelling.

But that was only in the background, and he was

sure no one else was paying attention. He was certain they were all paying attention to him and Jill.

Steven and Jill, he thought, grinning as he suavely handed Jill a menu. *Steven and Jill. Cool.* "The Razzamatazz burger's pretty decent," he told Jill. "It's, like, half a pound of beef, two kinds of cheese, Canadian bacon, steak fries, double onion rings, salsa, jalapeno peppers if you want 'em." He licked his lips in anticipation. The Razzamatazz was his usual order at the Dairi Burger. "And the shakes are truly awesome."

Jill shuddered delicately. "Oh, that sounds a little too rich for me," she said, laying her menu down and blinking up at him. "I think I'll just have a garden salad. With low-fat dressing. And do they have sparkling water?"

Steven honestly didn't know. Somehow, the question had never come up. "Um—" he said, frowning, as he ran his finger down the beverage list. Off to the side, the door to the ladies' room sprang open and Janet Howell stepped out.

Jill laughed her little tinkling laugh. "If they don't, then a Diet Sprite will do just fine," she said. "And if you'll excuse me for a moment, Steven . . . " She stood up and headed toward the ladies' room.

"OK," Steven said. He set the menu down and sat up a little straighter. He just knew everyone in the place was looking at him. *Wow*, they were probably thinking, *we had no idea Wakefield was so cool. But he must be, 'cause he's dating Jill Hale.* Steven nodded, satisfied. The news would probably be all over school on Monday. The Big Men and their crowd would probably notice him. McAndrew might even ask him to be lab partners in that chemistry class they were taking together. He might even get to sit in the front seats of the bus to the away basketball games instead of on the floor if there wasn't room . . .

Hold on, Wakefield, Steven told himself with a laugh. *You're getting a little ahead of yourself there. It's just your first date, after all.*

But it wasn't just their first real date. Already Steven could tell it was the start of something new. Something big. He was about to become a player at SVHS. Someone kids noticed. Looked up to. The epitome of cool, not like he'd been when he was just going out with Cathy.

Cathy. Steven bit his lip. Once again he wondered if he'd treated her well, just leaving her in the movie. He took a deep breath.

I'll call her, he said, standing up quickly before he could change his mind. *She's probably at home pining away for me. I'll just call and let her down easy.*

Of course it was the right thing to do. After all, if he was breaking up with her it would be nice to tell her so himself. In person. Before she started hearing it from other people. Grabbing the telephone, he dialed the number he knew so well.

"Hello?" The voice sounded down.

"Hi, Cathy," Steven said. "It's, um, me." He

paused. Just how did you say you wanted to break up—in a nice way, of course?

"Oh. You." The faintest whisper of a sigh drifted across the phone line and into Steven's ear.

Steven plunged ahead. "Listen, Cath," he began, "I've been thinking. About us, you know. And I've been thinking that—I mean—" *What have I been thinking anyway?* "That we should, like, break up. Maybe not forever," he added quickly in case Cathy got the wrong idea. "And it's not you. I still care about you and everything. But I just, you know, need to find myself, I guess." He cleared his throat. "Play the field and stuff."

Cathy was silent for a moment. Then she took a deep breath. "I see."

"It's not you, really it isn't," Steven assured her. He looked around the corner of the phone booth, making sure that Jill hadn't yet emerged from the bathroom. "We'll just have to see how all this shakes out," he said. "But—you wouldn't want me to sacrifice my own happiness, would you?"

There was silence. "No, I wouldn't," Cathy said slowly. "Only there are my own feelings to consider too, and—"

The door to the ladies' room clicked open and a vision of loveliness stepped out. *Jill.* Steven could feel his heart beginning to thump. "Talk to you later, Cath," he said, and hung up.

He felt a little like a jerk.

But only a little, he decided, as Jill flashed a brilliant smile right at him.

Six

◇

"Oh, Steven, you're so *funny!*" Jill giggled.

Steven raised his eyebrows. He hadn't thought the story he'd just told was so hilarious, but he wasn't about to argue with success. He took a swig of 7UP and grinned across the little table at Jill. "Yeah, well," he said modestly.

They were at the skating rink, taking a breather. In the background lights flashed, illuminating the floor in bright reds and greens, but Steven barely noticed. He was too busy staring at Jill, trying hard to memorize every single little detail about her. He couldn't believe his good luck. *After all*, he told himself, *when was the last time Cathy looked at me like that and said, "Oh, Steven, you're so* funny"? *Like, never.*

Steven pushed his chair back and stood up, noticing the way Jill sat with the back of her elbow just barely resting against the table. It was pretty cute, he decided. But then, almost everything about Jill was pretty cute. Starting with her perfect hair, and her perfect teeth, and her perfect skin, and her—"Want to, you know, skate some more?" Steven asked.

Jill giggled. "Oh, maybe in a little while," she said, turning up the corners of her mouth into a perfect smile. She rested her hand gently on Steven's. "Right now," she cooed, "I'd rather just sit here and talk to you."

"You would?" Steven swallowed hard. Had he died and gone to heaven? "I mean, OK," he added quickly, sliding his skates back under the table and sitting down with a thump. "If you want to."

"Oh, I do," Jill said. She fixed him with a look. "I just think we ought to get to know each other better," she purred.

Steven tried hard not to faint. He couldn't imagine what he had ever done to deserve this. But he wasn't about to complain. "Um—sure," he said suavely, dropping his voice an octave or so. "Whatever you say, Jill. I—I think I'd like to get to know you better too."

"I'm so glad we agree!" Jill said, breaking into that little tinkling laugh Steven liked so much. She hitched her chair nearer to the table. "So what do you think about the royal family in England? Wasn't it such a shame about the poor princess?"

Steven couldn't have possibly cared less about the poor princess. All he cared about was Jill's beautiful face floating less than a foot from his nose. "Oh, yeah," he said with feeling. "Like you said." He swallowed hard. Jill's face was a work of art, he decided, trying not to stare too obviously.

Jill's mouth opened, and she trilled that laugh again. Steven swooned at the sight of those beautiful teeth. "Personally, I think she deserved a better deal, don't you?"

Steven nodded. His heart beat faster.

"But now she's free to date anyone she wants." Jill broke into a huge grin. "That's the way it ought to be, Steven, don't you think so?" She stroked his arm gently.

"It sure is," Steven agreed. He stared deeply into Jill's eyes, basking in the feeling of her hand on his elbow. "You got that part right!"

See, Howell! he exulted, though he knew Howell wasn't even in the building. *And you thought I was such a one-woman man. Well, I'm not.* Impulsively he took Jill's hand in his own. He breathed deeply. It felt warm. Fresh. As if it belonged there.

Jill batted her eyelashes and giggled again.

No doubt about it, Steven decided. *It's good for me to get out once in a while with somebody besides—*

Besides—

He searched his mind. Cathy, that was it. Of course.

But it was funny how hard it was to remember her name at a time . . . like . . . this . . .

*   *   *

"So what are we going to do about the dance?" Jessica demanded. She faced Elizabeth in the Wakefields' living room, hands on her hips. "We just can't not have dates!"

Elizabeth didn't quite meet her sister's gaze. "I hear you, Jess," she said. "It's just that—" She stole a quick look at the clock hanging on the wall. "It's past ten o'clock, and we really don't have to do it today, and I don't even think it's—" Her voice trailed off. *So important*, she'd been going to say, but that wasn't the best thing to tell Jessica just now.

"Listen." Jessica stabbed a forefinger in Elizabeth's direction. "Do you or do you not agree that those are two of the most dreamy guys in the entire world?"

Elizabeth nodded slowly. "But can't it wait till tomorrow, Jessica?" she asked. "I mean, it's so late."

Jessica rolled her eyes. "My sister is a wimp," she announced to no one in particular. "A total wimpface! What are you going to do—sit around and *wait* for Todd to change his mind?"

Elizabeth blushed. "Not exactly," she said. She wished Jessica weren't quite so—so determined. Arguing with Jessica was like trying to keep an ice cube cold in an oven set to three hundred and fifty degrees. She yawned. "I'm just so tired."

Jessica snorted. "You know what Todd's going to wind up like in a few years," she threatened. "Steven Wakefield, Junior. *I'm* sure not waiting around to see Aaron turn into a jerk like our famous brother."

Elizabeth shook her head. She knew what her sister meant. A picture of her brother holding hands with Jill sprung into her mind. *Ugh, gross.* "It's just that—" But she could feel herself beginning to give in.

"Remember how he said, 'After you?'" Jessica made little mincing steps. "'After you. After you,'" she said in a silly voice. "He goes out with Cathy, who's, like, the greatest person on earth, practically, and he comes back with Jill Hale, who's the pits. He treats Cathy like dirt, and he treats Jill like she's queen of the universe. And that'll happen to you too," she continued, her eyes narrowing. "One day you'll walk into a movie theater with Todd and he'll walk out with—" She hesitated.

"With Cammi Adams," Elizabeth said half under her breath. Maybe Cammi was just borrowing Todd's notes or something, or going over the assignment with him to be sure she'd written it down right. Then again, maybe not.

She sighed. It *was* late, too late to be going to the Claybaughs' house.

But Jessica could be awfully persuasive.

And the brothers were awfully cute.

And maybe it *was* time to teach Todd a lesson. Especially if he was thinking about going *anywhere* with Cammi.

"All right, Jess," she sighed. "Let's go back to Pete's."

"Steven?" Jill dipped her head and smiled. "How about another 7UP?"

"Oh—sure," Steven stammered. He released Jill's hand and struggled to his feet. "Um—be right back." It was hard to tear his eyes away from Jill's face, even after she'd stopped looking at him and was busy studying her fingernails.

With quick sweeping strokes Steven skated over to the concession stand. *Hmm.* Out of the corner of his eye, Steven thought he saw someone familiar on the other side of the skating rink. The hair, the eyes, the way she skated.

Cathy. He nodded slowly. Yup, it was definitely Cathy. For a fraction of a second he felt butterflies in his stomach.

Slowing to a stop, he looked closer. Cathy was an awfully good skater, he had to admit. Better than Jill anyway. Jill really wasn't much of a skater when you came right down to it. He grinned. Maybe that was why she didn't seem to be interested in going back to the skating floor.

Or maybe she just wanted to spend some private time alone with him. Yeah. He stood up a little straighter and adjusted the collar of his shirt. *She wants to get to know me better. And she can't do that on a crowded skating rink surface.*

Jill was so cute and fun, he couldn't imagine why they hadn't gotten together before this. He sighed and got in line at the concession booth. *Chemistry*, he told himself. *Yeah, chemistry. That's what we've got, Jill and me.*

He took a quick glance over his shoulder. There

was Cathy, weaving in and out of the skaters with a big smile on her face. Behind her he recognized a couple of her best friends. *Good,* he thought. Cathy didn't seem too broken up about what had happened. Not anymore anyway.

On the other hand—

"Yeah?" the kid behind the counter said. "What do you want?"

"Um—one 7UP, please," Steven said, digging in his pocket for his wallet. This evening was going to cost him, that was for sure. This was about the sixth soft drink he'd bought. To say nothing of the burgers earlier. And, of course, the movie tickets for himself and Cathy to begin the evening—

He frowned. Cathy had to be just a *little* broken up about what he'd done, he decided. It wouldn't be, like, normal if she wasn't. He looked back at the rink. Cathy was whizzing by. She had a big grin on her face still, but Steven thought he noticed a little sadness in her eyes. He nodded.

"Here you go," the kid said, handing Steven a plastic cup and a straw.

"Thanks," Steven said. He turned and glided back toward the table. Of course she was sad, he told himself. He knew Cathy, and he could tell. He couldn't help feeling just a little sorry for her. After all, the fact that she was here at the rink enjoying herself with her friends didn't mean she wasn't pining away for him inside.

She's so brave that way, he told himself, the wheels

of his skates digging into the hardwood floor.

But that was history. He and Cathy were through being steady dates. Tonight he was with Jill.

Cathy was definitely fun. But Jill. Now Jill was something else again. Jill was . . .

Well. He considered. Jill was Jill.

"We could yell, 'Fire,'" Jessica suggested. There was no sign of the brothers at Pete's house. There didn't even seem to be any lights on.

Elizabeth shuddered. "No thanks!" she said.

"What are you going to do, wait all your life?" Jessica bit off the words. "You'll be, like, ninety-three before you're even invited to the high school prom. Anyway, what's the harm?"

"Of shouting 'Fire'?" Elizabeth stared at Jessica in astonishment. "Lots of harm. Anyway, they're probably in bed. Come on, Jessica, let's just go home."

Jessica scowled. The brothers were not either in bed, she was certain. They were someplace else. Being introduced to somebody.

No. Jessica's scowl deepened. Being introduced to *two* somebodies. Probably—Janet and Lila. Janet, because Janet's brother Joe was sort of a friend of Pete's also, only Joe was a nice enough guy that he might actually *do* something for his sister once in a while, and Lila because—because it was the kind of lucky thing that always seemed to happen to Lila Fowler. "I'm going to do it," she whispered, half hoping that Elizabeth would talk her out of it. She rose up behind the bushes.

"Jess!" Elizabeth grabbed her sister's sleeve. "You can't!"

"Oh, yeah?" In her mind's eye Jessica saw Janet talking excitedly with the older cousin, on the other side of the house where the lights didn't show.

"Fire!" she yelled.

"Hey, Cathy!" Steven signaled to her from the entrance to the skating floor. Jill had left him for a few minutes to go freshen up in the ladies' room, and he was beginning to feel a little guilty about what he'd done to Cathy.

Cathy skated to the wall and stopped expertly on one foot. "What do you want?" she asked.

"To apologize," Steven said grandly. It felt good to get it off his chest. "I wanted to say, you know, I'm sorry and all that. I know you must be really crying inside."

"Huh?" Cathy looked blank.

Steven frowned. That wasn't supposed to be her reaction. *The poor, poor kid. She's probably so upset her heart's shut down.* "I feel terrible about it, but, hey, a man's gotta do what a man's gotta do." It had been one of the few complete lines of dialogue from *Danger Zone, Part Six.*

Cathy kept staring at him.

For crying out loud, Cath, would you say something? "I wish there was more than one of me so you wouldn't have to be alone," he went on. "But, you know, it's cruel irony and the hand of fate and it's as painful for me as it is for you," he finished, trying to look miserable.

"Oh, *painful*." Cathy nodded. Her body turned, and her left skate bit angrily into the wood of the floor. Before Steven quite realized what was happening, Cathy's hip had sent him spinning into the wooden wall of the rink.

"Ow!" Steven winced. A flicker of pain shot through his toes where they'd collided with the wall.

"Wait up, guys!" Cathy cried cheerfully, waving to her friends and weaving quickly through the lines of skaters.

"I told you so," Elizabeth hissed from her hideout under the spreading branches of a pine tree. She knew from the start that coming back to the Claybaughs' was a stupid idea—and that Jessica's yelling "Fire!" was even stupider.

"Well, how was I supposed to know they weren't even *home?*" Jessica whispered.

Elizabeth gritted her teeth. No one had even come out of the Claybaughs' house after Jessica had yelled, but several neighbors had run out frantically, each thinking their own houses were the ones that were burning.

"No sign of any problem," a firefighter called out from outside the protective boughs.

I am never ever listening to Jessica again, Elizabeth thought, curling herself in a tight ball to avoid the beam of the firefighter's flashlight.

Seven

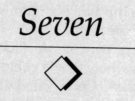

"Hello?" Wearily, Jessica picked up the phone. It was Saturday morning, and she hadn't slept well the night before. "Hi, Jessica." Jessica drew in her breath, recognizing Janet Howell's voice. "Roaches, huh?"

"Oh, the roaches," Jessica said with a nervous giggle. *Oops.* "Um, well, we kind of just jumped to conclusions," she lied. She was glad Janet couldn't see her face, which she was positive was turning bright red. "It was Elizabeth's fault, mostly. You see—"

"Save it, Jessica," Janet grumbled. "Denny wasn't there, and he swears he hasn't been anywhere near Ellen, so it's OK. Anyway, I wanted to invite you to my brother's band practice for the so-called street dance." She spoke the words with disdain.

The so-called street dance. Jessica smiled and breathed more easily. That probably meant Janet didn't have a date yet. Which probably meant she hadn't met the gorgeous brothers.

"You can bring your sister too, if you want," Janet said. "So you coming or not?"

"Sure," Jessica said, accepting for both herself and Elizabeth. She thanked Janet and hummed as she put the receiver down. So the brothers were still a possibility. Excellent.

"Hey, Joe, what happened to all the electronic stuff you used to play?" Ellen Riteman asked later that morning.

Joe shrugged and took his guitar off his shoulder. He was sweating heavily. "Oh, we just decided to go unplugged for a while," he said casually. "We just, you know, wanted to make a musical statement."

"Plus which, the amp broke and it costs too much to get a new one," the drummer said.

Elizabeth smiled. She had to admit, the band wasn't half bad. She was looking forward to hearing them play for real at the dance.

"Of course, what's the point of having a street dance if none of the really cool guys are going?" Ellen moaned. "The only guys left are geeks and nerds like Winston."

"And Randy Mason." Kimberly Haver held her nose.

Jessica grinned. Elizabeth's heart flip-flopped. She'd seen that grin before. "It just so happens that not *all* the really cool kids are going to the game," Jessica said.

"Like who?" Ellen frowned.

Jessica narrowed her eyes. "*We* have dates for the dance." She draped an arm around Elizabeth's shoulder.

"You do not either," Janet said scornfully.

"Sure do," Jessica promised.

"Who?" Kimberly put her hands on her hips.

"*Mystery* dates," Jessica said. She placed a finger against her lips and smiled. "It's a secret. You're just going to have to find out at the dance."

"But, Jessica—" Elizabeth began.

Jessica's hand tightened on Elizabeth's shoulder. Elizabeth understood the gesture all too well. It meant, "Don't say a word if you know what's good for you!"

"Yeah, right," Ellen said, taking a quick look at Janet. "You're just making it up. Isn't she, Janet?"

"I'm telling the truth," Jessica insisted.

Janet searched Jessica's face. "OK," she said after a moment. "We'll make a bet. If you show up with those dates, I'll—" She considered. "I'll say my brother's band is better than Johnny Buck's."

"At the street dance?" Jessica wanted to know.

Janet nodded. "Into the microphone. But if you're lying, then you two have to show up dressed exactly alike."

Elizabeth drew in her breath. She looked at the ground, hoping against hope that Jessica wouldn't be foolish enough to take the bet.

"*And*," Janet continued, looking meaningfully at Elizabeth, "you'll have to dance every dance together. Every single dance."

Elizabeth wasn't too crazy about that idea. She turned her face pleadingly to Jessica.

"You're on!" Jessica said brightly, her hand digging into Elizabeth's shoulder so hard now it hurt.

Janet's eyes sparkled. "You're my witnesses," she remarked, turning to the other Unicorns.

Shaking off Jessica's hand, Elizabeth turned to face her sister. "What are you *thinking* about?" she hissed.

"Relax," Jessica assured her. "I've got it all taken care of."

Elizabeth shook her head, feeling slightly exasperated. She didn't believe her sister for a moment.

"Hi, guys!" Lila Fowler walked through the garage door, grinning widely. "Hey, you'll never guess what I just saw in the pharmacy!" She winked at Janet. "Or, maybe I should say, *who*."

"Who?" Janet repeated, puzzled. "What do you mean, Lila?"

"Oh, nothing." Lila stood still, looking as if she was enjoying being the center of attention. "Just two of the absolutely most to-die-for boys in the entire history of the world, that's all." She waved her hand dismissively. "Not that any of *you* guys would be interested in *that*."

Jessica's face went white.

Elizabeth smiled grimly and shook her head.

She felt a little guilty about how much she enjoyed watching Jessica's reaction.

But, considering how her sister had taken that stupid bet, only a little.

"Who are they?" Janet demanded.

"What are their names?" Ellen asked.

"Where do they live?" Kimberly wanted to know. The Unicorns surged around Lila.

"Hey, don't knock me over!" Lila commanded. "I didn't get that far," she admitted. "They were just leaving when I came in, and—"

Well, thank goodness for small favors, Jessica thought. She relaxed a little. She still had an edge on the others. But she'd have to work fast now.

Correction. She and *Elizabeth* would have to work fast now. Especially after making that bet.

"Well, Lila has dibs on one of them," Janet admitted. She put her hands on her hips and stared daggers at Kimberly. "Because she saw them first. But I get the other because I'm president of the Unicorn Club."

"But what if he doesn't *like*—" Ellen began.

"Of course he'll like me," Janet snapped. "Why wouldn't he like me?" She stared at Ellen, challenging her to answer the question.

"Oh," Ellen stammered. "I meant—well—"

The garage door opened again. Jessica's heart sank as Pete Claybaugh walked in.

"Hey, Howell, my man!" Pete greeted Joe.

Jessica held her breath and followed Pete. She had to make sure he didn't say anything stupid. Like, about cousins. *Don't talk about the boys*, she urged him silently.

"Claybaugh. How you doing?" Joe nodded to Pete.

Pete grinned. "Can't complain."

Joe fingered some chords on his guitar. "You're just in time. Want to hear us do Johnny Buck's latest big hit?"

"Sure," Pete said, nodding slowly. "Hey, you know who knows all the Buckster's songs by heart? One of my *cousins*, man. He's, like, twelve and he already—"

Jessica's blood froze. Not daring to wait another moment, she did the only thing she could: dive into the drum set. "Ow!" she yelled as drums, cymbals, and mallets crashed all around her.

"Oh, *Jessica*," Janet said in a voice that oozed disapproval.

"What a klutz," Joe said under his breath. "Listen," he said, raising his voice, "all middle-school kids get out of here, OK? This is serious business and we need quiet."

"But, Joe—" Janet protested.

"I said out," Joe growled, pointing to the door with his guitar. He glared at Jessica, then reluctantly offered her a hand up.

"Th-thanks," Jessica panted. Her hip hurt from landing on the floor. "I'm, like, really sorry. I guess somebody must have knocked into me. Probably

Elizabeth," she added, staring daggers at her sister. "Want me to help put it back together?"

"Ah, forget it," Joe said, shaking his head. "Just get out."

Jessica nodded. She *was* sorry. Also in pain, and also embarrassed.

But in spite of it all, she was feeling pretty good. She'd gotten the Unicorns away from Pete, and her secret was still safe.

For now.

"That's funny." Elizabeth frowned. The twins were on their way down the Howells' driveway toward the street.

"What's strange?" Jessica wanted to know.

Elizabeth didn't answer. Cathy Connors was coming toward them. Without saying anything, Cathy waved at the twins and walked through the door of the garage. *Funny,* Elizabeth thought. *Cathy doesn't usually hang with these kids, does she?*

"I don't get it," Jessica complained.

Elizabeth narrowed her eyes and stared through the now open door to the garage. The band hadn't started its next number yet, and Cathy was deep in conversation with Joe.

Elizabeth frowned. It didn't make sense. Joe and Cathy barely knew each other, really. Their only connection was Steven, and now that Steven and Cathy were history, what was—

"Come *on*," Jessica said, tugging at Elizabeth's

arm. "We'd better go find the brothers before You-Know-Who beats us to it."

Elizabeth shook her off. Inside the garage, Cathy and Joe were still talking. "Shh," she whispered. But even with Jessica quiet at her side, she still couldn't make out any words. Joe looked a little upset, that much she could tell.

"Elizabeth!" Jessica stamped her foot impatiently. "Get a move on."

Joe grinned and gave Cathy a thumbs-up signal. Reluctantly Elizabeth tore her eyes away from the open door.

Probably it doesn't mean anything, she told herself as she followed her sister down the block. *They're just talking, is all.*

But the question bothered her all the way to the Claybaughs'.

Eight

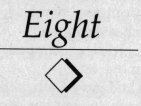

"Hey, Wakefield! You home?"

Reluctantly, Steven pulled himself away from the bathroom mirror. It was Sunday evening. He'd been trying to cover over a zit with a little baby powder, but it didn't seem to be working. "That you, Joe?" he called downstairs. *Mom must have let him in. . . .*

"Yeah." Joe's face appeared at the bottom of the staircase. "Listen, I just wanted to borrow your algebra book if you're not going to be using it—" He stopped and stared. "Whoa! What's with the tie?"

"The tie?" Steven glanced down at the tie he'd borrowed from his dad for his big date that evening. Stroking it gently, he held it out to Joe for inspection. "Not bad, huh? I've got me a big date for tonight." He winked conspiratorially at Joe, hoping he looked really cool. *Jill probably will say I'm, like, incredibly handsome,* he told himself proudly. He didn't usually get dressed up like this, but for Jill some fancy clothes were worth the discomfort.

"A big date?" Joe narrowed his eyes. "Hey, listen, buddy, have I heard this right? You and Cathy have, like, busted up?"

Steven grinned. "Yeah," he admitted, dropping his eyes modestly to the floor. "It just wasn't, you know, working out. For either of us. So my big date tonight's with—" He adjusted his tie and put his shoulders back. "With Jill Hale."

"Oh." Joe looked thoughtful.

You're supposed to say, Wow, Steven thought, a little annoyed at Joe's reaction. *I mean, this is Jill Hale. The big time, you know?* "Third night in a row too. Friday, burgers and skating. Saturday, bowling and pizza. Tonight, the dance club. So I guess you were wrong about me being a one-woman kind of a guy," he boasted. "I mean, maybe Cathy and I'll get back together someday, but this just isn't the right time."

Joe nodded slowly. "OK," he said after a moment. "Well, you know, Steven, if you and Cathy are really through, then—" He paused and narrowed his eyes.

"Then what?" Steven asked, curious.

"Then you wouldn't mind if I asked her out, would you?" Joe went on, as if he were thinking out loud. "If she's free and everything." He shrugged elaborately.

Steven froze. He saw Joe and Cathy in his

mind's eye, strolling hand in hand down the side-walks of Sweet Valley, sharing a sundae at Casey's, skating together—doing all the things that he and Cathy used to do. He felt a twinge of jealousy. *I think I do mind,* he said to himself.

But of course he couldn't say that. Not with Jill waiting to be taken to the dance club. Not after picking out the tie. Not after seeing the pain in Cathy's eyes at the roller rink. He just couldn't hurt her like that. If Joe wanted to try his luck, who was Steven to stop him?

"Sure," he said slowly. "Fair's fair. If I'm dating Jill, I guess I shouldn't try to keep Cathy from dating somebody else."

Dating Jill. The words had a nice ring to them. He grinned. Yeah. Dumping Cathy was for the best.

Joe grinned back. "Good," he said. "Then I'll call her sometime."

Steven nodded, slowly at first, then faster.

I've hurt Cathy, after all, he told himself. *And it wouldn't be fair to keep her from finding happiness with—someone else.*

If she can.

Despite himself, Steven grinned. He'd have to peg the odds of Joe and Cathy getting together at less than zero.

Way, *way* less than zero.

"This is such a cool place!" Jill squealed. "Do you come here often?"

"Well—" Steven hesitated. In fact, he'd only been to the club once, with Cathy. They'd always talked about going back, but never had. Now they probably never would. "Once or twice," he said with a casual shrug. "You?"

Jill smiled and leaned closer to him on the bench beside the dance floor. Nearby, other kids whirled and spun. "Oh, I come here all the time," she told him with a giggle. "I came here with Bobby Peters, and Frank Patrick, and Richard Ferris, and Kevin McAndrew, and—" She made a face. "But best of all I like coming here with you."

Steven smiled. She'd named a whole bunch of the Big Men, though the only one he really knew at all was Ferris. He was totally psyched to be mentioned in the same breath with those guys. "Come on, let's dance," he suggested, half rising from his seat. They hadn't actually danced much so far.

Jill looked surprised. "Oh, not just yet, Steven," she said, casting her eyes around the room and fussing with her hair. "Let's just stay here and talk!"

"Oh." Slowly Steven sat down. "OK. Um—what do you want to talk about?"

"Oh, whatever," Jill said lightly. "What do you think of, let me see, lemon juice?"

Lemon juice? Steven frowned. "What do you mean?" he asked. "It's, like, kind of sour to drink, isn't it?"

"For your hair, silly!" Jill laughed and shook her head, letting her hair shimmer in the lights. "See those blond places? I rub lemon juice on them every day before I go out in the sun," she told him proudly.

"Gee, that's great." Steven honestly didn't know what else to say. He ran his hand up and down the arm of the bench. One thing was for sure, Jill did like to talk a lot. In three hours at the bowling alley last night they'd managed to get in just two games.

"And another way to get blond highlights," Jill went on, "at least my cousin told me all about this, but I don't know if it's true, is you take a whole big tea bag and empty it out into a wet Kleenex, and then you press the Kleenex against your hair for, like, two hours, and that's what she *says* but I don't know if it's true. What do you think, Steven?"

"Um—yeah," Steven said, thoroughly confused by now. "I mean—no. Well—"

"Oh, and there's a way that uses bananas too," Jill went on. She screwed up her face and sighed thoughtfully. "Did you know that there's a really important nutrient that you only get in banana peels? I forget what it is, but if you don't get it you, like, shrivel up and die." She waved a forefinger at him warningly. "So make sure you eat a lot of banana peels, OK?"

"Banana peels?" Steven shook his head. "Listen, do you want to dance now?" he asked hopefully.

"Of course, banana peels," Jill burbled, looking at him reproachfully. "I read all about in *More Beautiful You* magazine. It's one of the biggest health problems in this country today."

Steven was almost certain that he had personally never eaten a banana peel in his entire life, and he was in pretty darn good health. At least, he thought he was. But he flexed a bicep just to make sure. He grinned. "What do they call it—vitamin Y deficiency?" he asked.

"Huh?" Jill stared at him as if he came from outer space.

"Joke," Steven explained. "You know, like, vitamin Y? Y for yellow, and banana skins are yellow?" It was sort of feeble, he had to admit. "Ha ha and all that?"

Jill frowned. "Oh," she said. "You were making a joke. I get it." But she didn't laugh or even smile.

Steven sighed. Not only did Jill talk too much and never seem to want to *do* anything, she didn't have much of a sense of humor either. *Cathy would have laughed at that,* he told himself, and immediately felt ashamed for thinking about Cathy when he was with Jill, the girl of his dreams.

"Jill!" A junior girl approached their bench. Steven didn't know her very well, but recognized her as one of the most popular girls in school. "What have you done with your nails?" she asked enthusiastically.

"Like them?" Jill wanted to know. She waved her hands this way and that, admiring the colors. "I mixed together three different shades of polish: Midnight Magenta, Pale Pink Amaryllis, and Dull Rose."

"They're beautiful!" the older girl said. "Listen, Jill, I'm having a party next week at my house, and I was wondering if you'd like to come."

Jill trilled a little laugh and ran her hand gently

across Steven's shoulder. "I'd love to!" she said.

A party? Steven knew better than to ask if he was invited too, but he hoped he would be. That would be the ultimate in the SVHS social scene. "Um—hi," he said huskily, sticking out his hand. "I'm, um, Steven. Wakefield."

"Sally," the girl said, not offering her hand in return. "You can come if you want. I guess. Hey, Jill, I thought you were dating—"

"Oh, that's all over now," Jill interrupted, winding her arm around the back of Steven's neck. "*Some* people appreciate me and some . . . just don't." She smiled at Steven. "*Some* people don't think it's so cool just to go off and play the field."

"Uh-huh," Steven said proudly, wondering what Jill was talking about. "Thanks, Sally. I'd, um, love to come."

"I'll call you with the details," Sally told Jill, not looking at Steven. "And you can pass them on to *him*." She jerked a shoulder in Steven's direction. "Catch you later."

"Sally's parties are so much fun," Jill said affectionately, ruffling Steven's hair. "Oh—isn't that—"

"Who?" Steven turned around to see.

"Nobody," Jill sniffed, shifting in her seat. "Nobody worth knowing just now anyway."

Steven frowned. Coming toward him were five of the Big Men, led by Richard Ferris. *The coolest guys in the school*, Steven reminded himself. Why would Jill be so upset? "Hey, guys!" he called out, feeling important.

"Wakefield." Ferris stopped and extended his hand. "How are things?" His eyes flicked past Steven and onto Jill, who was staring hard in the other direction.

"Hey, Wakefield," Johnston said. "How you doing?"

"We're just fine," Steven said, deciding it was important to show the guys that he and Jill were together. He reached out to stroke the back of Jill's neck. "Having fun?"

Ferris nodded slowly. "Stay cool," he said. "See you around, Jill." He sketched a wave and moved on without waiting for an answer.

"He's so awesome, isn't he?" Steven murmured, watching the Big Men walk away. His heart was soaring. Imagine, a freshman like him having a real conversation with a guy like Ferris. He guessed that Ferris was mostly impressed because Steven was now dating Jill, but he didn't even care.

"Oh, I don't know," Jill said in a thin voice. "If you like that sort of thing."

Steven wondered once more what was eating Jill, but he decided he wouldn't worry too much about it. Proudly he reached for her hand. Dating Jill was the best decision he'd ever made. She was absolutely gorgeous, even if she wasn't the most fun person he'd ever met in his life. And she was nice in her own way, and . . . and . . .

Steven smiled to himself. And she was his ticket to major coolness at Sweet Valley High.

*   *   *

"We could make a phone call," Jessica suggested glumly. It was Sunday night, and the twins were sitting at the kitchen table.

"I guess so," Elizabeth agreed halfheartedly. "You could anyway."

Jessica grimaced. Things were getting worse and worse. The girls hadn't even caught a glimpse of Pete's cousins since that night in the Dairi Burger. They'd staked out the sporting goods and comic books stores at the mall; they'd hung out at the Dairi Burger most of Saturday night, hoping the boys would return for another "pretty decent" sundae or two; and they'd walked back and forth in front of Pete's house so many times Jessica thought they might be about to wear a path in the sidewalk.

Yet the brothers hadn't showed up. Not even once.

"But what would we *say*?" Elizabeth murmured.

"We'd *say*, 'Hello, Pete, I'd like to speak to your cousins, please,'" Jessica said sulkily. "I mean, 'I'd like to speak to your older cousin.' I mean—" She shook her head. It was tough calling someone when you didn't even know his name.

"And if the cousin came to the phone after all, what would you say then?" Elizabeth asked curiously.

Jessica scowled and slumped across the table. "I'd say—um—" She rubbed her eyes tiredly. *"You're incredibly gorgeous and I'd love to meet you"* just didn't seem right, somehow. *"You don't know me, and you don't know what you're missing"* sounded even worse.

"We should just give it up," Elizabeth suggested, nibbling a pencil. "After all—"

"Give it up?" Jessica raised her head, scarcely believing what she was hearing. "Are you out of your *gourd* or what? Of course we can't give it up!" Visions of dancing with Elizabeth all night long filled her mind. Visions of Janet's victorious face filled her mind too. "Give me that phone!" Her heart was beating so fast she thought it might pop out of her chest.

"You're going to do it?" Elizabeth's eyes opened wide.

"I just said so, didn't I?" Jessica snapped. "Where's that number?" She knew she'd have to work fast—before she lost her nerve. She scrambled for the phone book, located the number, and punched it in with a shaky finger. "Shh," she hissed to Elizabeth as the phone began to ring.

"I didn't say a word," Elizabeth protested.

"That has nothing to do with it!" Jessica hissed. *Two rings—three.* There was a click. "Hello?" came a woman's voice.

"Um—hello." Jessica stiffened. Maybe it would be safer to go through Pete. "Is, um, Pete there, please?"

There was a pause. "I'm afraid Pete is busy studying," Mrs. Claybaugh told her. "Is it important? Who shall I say is calling?"

Jessica's mouth felt dry. "Tell him, it's, um, a

friend," she said. "And, it's, like, real important," she added. *Like, a matter of life and death.*

There was a sigh. "One moment, please," Mrs. Claybaugh said. In the background Jessica could hear a muffled yell: "Pete! Phone. It's a girl. No, she won't tell me her name."

"What's going on?" Elizabeth hissed.

Jessica put her finger to her lips. An extension picked up. "H'lo?" Pete barked.

Jessica's stomach was full of gigantic butterflies. "Um, hi, Pete," she said. "Um—how are you?"

"Fine," Pete said. "Who's this?"

Jessica took a deep breath. Did she dare or didn't she dare? No, she definitely did not dare. "Um—a friend," she said. "Um, Pete, I, I really wanted to talk to, um, one of your cousins."

"My cousins?" Pete sounded disbelieving. "You mean one of the *kids?*" There was a pause. "Hey, who is this anyway?"

Jessica escaped having to answer by pretending to have a huge coughing fit. "Please, Pete," she said in a shaky voice when she came up for air, "I really need to know—"

"Listen." Pete sounded firm. "I'm not an answering machine, OK? I've got a humongous Spanish test tomorrow, and if I don't pass I'm off the basketball team, got that? I told Mom that the only people who could disturb me were, well—" He hesitated. "Not you anyway, whoever you are. Now get off the line and leave me alone." There was a click.

Jessica stared at the phone in her hand, then turned to Elizabeth.

"Well, do we have a Plan B?" she asked her sister with a sigh.

"Can you believe Mrs. Nicholas made me do a problem on the board during science today?" Jill demanded on Monday. "I practically broke a nail!"

The lunch table in the high school cafeteria erupted with sighs and sympathetic nods, but Steven just made a face.

There was a lot to be said for sitting with Jill and her friends, he knew. Like the social prestige. And the way half the guys in the school were looking at him with jealousy written all over their faces. And the fact that Jill was incredibly foxy.

"She just doesn't like girls with long nails," Jill's friend Sally said. "One time, when I'd just finished decorating mine, you know what she had the nerve to do?"

"Tell us!" Jill said, leaning forward with a horror-stricken look on her face.

Steven wrinkled his nose. On the other hand, the air was so thick with perfume he could hardly breathe. Strange as it sounded, he almost wished he was back at his usual table with—

"I tell you, Cathy," a very familiar voice said practically at his elbow. "I'm really happy we got together for lunch."

Steven's heart stopped. The voice was Joe's, no doubt about it. Steven drew in his breath sharply and turned to look. There, right next to the table, were Joe and Cathy—*holding hands*.

Steven's head swam. *Already?* he thought incredulously. Cathy couldn't be over him so soon. She couldn't be ready to start a new romance.

"Well, I'm so glad you called me last night," Cathy said simply.

Steven bit his lip. *The poor kid*, he thought. She must really be sobbing on the inside to be behaving like this. He wondered how he could go on with the knowledge that he'd brought so much pain on a girl who was as much fun as Cathy was.

"And the makeup!" Jill was saying. "I came to class one day with just a little blush and some base, oh, and some eyebrow pencil and some mascara, and of course lipstick, but not even *eye shadow*, and she looked at me like—"

And the worst of it was, Steven mused, her pain was his pain, and he was such a sensitive guy that the pain of breaking up with her was like, so painful, that he, well . . . He took a deep breath. The scent of Jill's perfume hit him like a ton of bricks, and he knew what he had to do.

I can't cause her this much distress, he told himself, watching with tight lips as Cathy and Joe strolled smiling across the cafeteria.

I just can't let her go on like this . . . so . . . unhappy.

Nine

◇

Feeling a little nervous, Steven rang the doorbell that he'd rung so many times before. He hoped Cathy was home.

It had taken him a while to get to Cathy's after school. First, he'd had to get rid of Jill, which hadn't been easy. They'd sat out front of the school, just talking, for what seemed like hours, while Ferris played basketball nearby with Patrick, McAndrew, Peters, and some of the other Big Men. Steven had wished he could have joined them. It would have been more interesting than listening to Jill talk about different brands of emery boards.

It wasn't that he was through with Jill, exactly, Steven reflected as he waited for the door to open. He was psyched to take her to Sally's party . . . and hopefully other parties too. But the street dance was sort of—well, sort of Cathy's property. He'd kind of promised her a while back.

Joe's face flashed briefly into his mind. Steven only hoped Cathy still remembered that sort-of promise.

There was movement behind the door. *She'll probably fall into my arms right away*, Steven told himself, grinning at the thought.

"Oh." Cathy opened the door and frowned. "It's you."

"That's right, Cathy," Steven said, putting a pained look on his face and sticking his foot into the doorway, just in case. *We'll hug and I'll share her pain and—*

"What do you want?" Cathy asked, narrowing her eyes. "Your CDs? I shipped them back to you already, FedEx." She started to close the door.

"Wait!" Steven said. His heart was thumping in his chest. "It's not the CDs, it's *you*," he said. *Stay cool, Wakefield, stay cool*, he urged himself. "I just—can't keep on hurting you like this." He swallowed hard. "I'm willing to, you know, let bygones be bygones, and take you to the—"

Street dance, he was going to say, but Cathy interrupted him. "I see," she said frostily, her eyes flashing. "Thanks very much, Steven, but you've hurt me enough already! Talk about insensitive and immature!"

"Cathy—" Steven stared at Cathy open-mouthed. "I'm trying to tell you—the street dance—"

"I don't care, Steven," Cathy said. "Who needs someone selfish like you hanging around? Now, as for Joe—" Her face broke into a smile, and she sighed dreamily. "He's kind and sweet and charming and—and everything you're not! I can't imagine how he can stand to be buddies with you!"

Steven threw his arms wide, scarcely believing what he was hearing. "For crying out loud, Cathy, I'm apologizing already!"

"Too late." Cathy grabbed the doorknob and pushed. "Thanks a lot for breaking up with me, because now I can go out with Joe. Now beat it!"

Steven considered leaving his foot in the doorway (it would show Cathy how much he was willing to share her pain all over again), but he narrowly pulled it back instead. Just in time. The door closed with such force that the hinges rattled.

Steven shook his head. He absolutely, positively, could not believe it. How could anybody, especially somebody with Cathy's good taste, prefer Joe Stupid Howell to Steven (the Great) Wakefield? "And I apologized too," he muttered, walking away from the door and staring up at Cathy's house.

He took a deep breath. Well, he wasn't going to let a little thing like rejection stop him. No way.

He was a one-woman man after all. His little separation from Cathy just proved it. He couldn't live without her. Jill was pretty cool, but hanging with her could do serious damage to your brain. And your lungs.

I'm going to get back with Cathy again, he promised himself.

If he could only figure out how . . .

The Claybaughs' front door swung open wide. "Yes?" Mrs. Claybaugh asked, smiling.

Jessica smiled back and held out her clipboard, hoping she looked suitably professional. It was Monday afternoon, and she and Elizabeth had hit on a perfect way to meet Pete's cousins. "Good afternoon, ma'am," she said brightly, trying hard not to sound like the dork who had called for Pete last night. "I'm Jessica and this is my sister, Elizabeth."

Mrs. Claybaugh frowned slightly and glanced over her shoulder. "You're not selling anything, are you? Because I'm a little low on cash at the moment and—"

"Oh, no, not selling anything," Jessica interrupted quickly. "We're conducting a poll."

"A poll?" Mrs. Claybaugh raised her eyebrows. "Oh, good! I just love polls."

Jessica took a deep breath. "Um, not you," she said aloud, hoping Mrs. Claybaugh wouldn't be too disappointed. "We're looking for a different, um, target demographic. Say—" She peered at the blank sheet of paper on her clipboard, trying to figure out how old Pete was so she could leave him out. "Say in the ten to fourteen age range."

"Boys," Elizabeth hissed.

"Males only, of course," Jessica added, wishing

her sister would speak up for herself once in a while.

"Oh, dear." Mrs. Claybaugh wrinkled her nose. "Too bad. We did have a couple of boys here who matched that description. My nephews, visiting from out of town. But they've gone home."

"Oh," Jessica said stupidly. She blinked hard. *Gone home? What right did they have to go home?*

"Oh," Elizabeth echoed. She stared at her twin as if to ask, "Now what?"

"Too bad," Mrs. Claybaugh told them. "But maybe you could use my input anyway. Do you have a category for age 35 to 39, female?"

Jessica shook her head. "Never mind," she muttered. "Thanks for your time." Turning, she tugged Elizabeth down the walk in front of her. Her whole body felt numb.

"I could try to answer your questions the way the boys would," Mrs. Claybaugh offered.

"Um—no thanks," Elizabeth said softly. "Sorry."

Jessica walked faster. No Claybaugh cousins. No chance of winning the bet.

She'd be the laughingstock of practically the whole school if she didn't do something quick. But what?

Steven couldn't believe the way Cathy had treated him. *And after all we've been through together too*, he thought glumly as he pushed open the front door of his house.

He bit his lip. But even after the way she'd slammed the door on him, he wasn't willing to give her up. No sirree. No, he wanted her back even more. At least for the street dance. And she wanted him back too. He was sure she'd rather go to the dance with him than with Howell, if she only knew it.

He paused on the stairs. The twins were in the living room, arguing.

"I can't believe you thought that would work!" Elizabeth was saying.

"Yeah, well, how was I supposed to know?" Jessica snapped back. "And I didn't notice you exactly doing anything to get us those dates!"

Typical girl behavior, Steven thought grimly. He began reflecting once more on the miserable way Cathy had treated him. And after all he'd done for her too. He sprawled on the couch, barely noticing his sisters.

Elizabeth leaned back in her chair and fixed Jessica with a look. "Anyway, I wasn't the one who made that stupid bet!"

"Yeah, you wouldn't have had the guts," Jessica jeered, folding her arms. "I don't know why I ever bothered to tell you about Pete's cousins. I should have kept them both for myself!"

Pete's cousins. Steven frowned. That was right; the girls had been trying to get dates with Pete's cousins earlier. It seemed like a long, long time ago.

"And besides—" Jessica went on when Elizabeth didn't speak.

Steven buried his face in the pillows of the couch. It sounded like they were having trouble connecting with the brothers on their own. He snorted. *Typical*, he thought again.

"Hey, you guys," he said, raising himself up on one elbow, "if you think you've got it bad, wait till you hear what happened to me! Remember Cathy?"

Jessica and Elizabeth exchanged glances. "How could we forget?" Jessica snapped. "You guys were only together for, like, months. Until you dumped her." She shot him an icy glare.

Steven felt his face turning red. "Well, I did what I thought was best," he said defensively. "Only it turned out not to be so best after all. Kind of. If you, um, know what I mean. And now she's treating me like—like dirt." Quickly he explained all the details—how he'd tried to make it up to her, how she wouldn't even listen, how she was dating Joe, how traumatized she must have been. Steven could feel himself getting more and more upset as he spoke. *We have to get back together again*, he thought mournfully. *We've got to!*

"So why are you telling us this, Steven?" Jessica interrupted, rolling her eyes.

"Yeah," Elizabeth chimed in. "If you're looking for sympathy, you've come to the wrong place."

"You dumped her, don't come crying to us," Jessica said snottily. "We always liked Cathy, remember. If you're a jerk, we can't exactly help that."

Steven shook his head. "I don't want your sympathy," he told them. "I just want—"

He hesitated. What had Jessica just said? *"We*

always liked Cathy, remember." The words rang in his ears. "I just want your help," he said slowly.

Because if Cathy wouldn't listen to him . . .

Maybe, just maybe, she'd listen to the twins.

"You want *us* to help *you?*" Jessica asked incredulously. "After you wouldn't help *us* get those dates with Pete's cousins?"

Elizabeth shook her head. If she lived to be two hundred and six, she decided, she would never understand her brother.

Swinging his legs over the edge of the couch pillows, Steven held up his hand. "You guys haven't gotten those dates yet, right? Those cousins of Claybaugh's?"

"No," Elizabeth admitted. "But that's because—"

"Well, listen up," Steven interrupted, smiling broadly and putting his hands casually on his hips. "You help me get Cathy back, and I'll arrange those dates for you."

"You'll—what?" Elizabeth could only stare. "But they've—"

"Details, details," Steven said, waving a hand in the air. "It's a done deal. I talked to Pete last night. All I gotta do is give him the go-ahead." He winked at the twins. "*Which* I'll do as soon as I get the go-ahead from you."

Elizabeth couldn't believe it. *He's lying through his teeth*, she thought. *How can he get us dates with guys who've gone home already?* She opened her mouth, about to tell Steven exactly what she thought of his so-called deal, but Jessica spoke first.

"Sure, Steven," she said calmly, giving Elizabeth a swift kick in the shins. "What exactly do you want us to do?"

Steven sighed with relief on his way up the stairs. Amazingly enough, the girls had agreed to his plan. He did feel a little ashamed at the way he'd fooled them. The truth was, he hadn't said word one to Claybaugh about fixing up the twins with dates for the dance. "But I *will* talk to him," he muttered to himself, walking into his room and pulling paper out of his desk drawer. "After this goes down. Probably, anyway."

Grinning, he sat down at his desk.

A little script, a movie screenplay, that was the ticket. A show starring himself. With the twins as supporting actresses. Not for nothing had he been a movie buff since the age of, like, two.

As for Jill, well, he'd take care of her later. After the street dance anyway. Maybe after Sally's party. He knew now he wasn't right for her and she wasn't right for him. But at the moment the big issue was getting Cathy back.

Steven looked down at the blank paper in front of him. His eyes flashed. *And if this plan doesn't bring Cathy back to me*, he told himself, *nothing will.*

Ten

◇

"OK, places!" Steven whispered.

It was Tuesday afternoon, and the three Wakefields were lying in wait for Cathy outside the pharmacy. Steven had seen her go in five minutes ago. Now he could see her through the heavy glass door, walking away from the checkout counter and toward the entrance.

Steven's mouth felt dry. *This better work,* he thought, darting back into the shadows.

But on the other hand, how can it possibly fail?

"Action!" he whispered, giving the signal to start just like a real movie director.

Cathy stepped out and blinked in the bright sunshine. Six feet in front of her, Jessica burst into tears. *Right on cue,* Steven thought proudly, pleased that his sister had such an ability to cry. "What's the matter, sis?" he asked in his most sensitive, caring voice. Trying to look worried, he walked to her side and put his arms around her.

Jessica sobbed harder. "I just—I just can't take it anymore," she hiccuped.

Steven lifted his head a fraction of an inch to make sure Cathy was watching. She was! His heart soared. "There, there, kid," he murmured soothingly, stroking Jessica's back. "You know you can count on me." *Stupid dialogue, but hey, whatever works, right?* "I'm your big brother, remember?"

He waited for Jessica to reply, but she didn't. "C'mon," he hissed under his breath. Had she forgotten her line? "You say, 'Oh, Steven, you're the only one who really understands.'"

But Jessica wrenched away from his grip. Sobbing, she turned to face Cathy. "Cut it out, Steven," she said through her tears. "You should know!"

"What are you talking about?" Steven stared at his sister in shock. "The script!" he hissed. "Um— I'm just trying to help—" he said aloud, improvising quickly.

Elizabeth stepped forward. "What did you do to her this time?" she demanded, reaching out to comfort Jessica. "I've asked you and asked you not to pick on her. Why don't you listen—for once in your life?"

"But—but I—" Steven bit his lip. Something had gone very, very wrong. The twins weren't following the script he'd written at all! *Of all the low-down, disgusting, rotten tricks to play—* His head swam. He longed to yell at them, but he knew that if he did, he'd blow the whole game.

"Like I *said*, Steven . . . " Elizabeth warned him.

Steven reached for the girls, putting on the very most sensitive smile he could possibly imagine. "Poor kids," he said sadly, looking directly at Cathy. "They're so—so confused these days—"

"Yeah, right," Elizabeth snapped. "You know that Jessica's going through a terrible time, no thanks to you. Now go away and leave us alone!"

"Steven Wakefield!" Cathy stamped her foot. Guiltily, Steven let go of his sisters. "I can't believe you're doing this! You're an even bigger creep than I thought!"

Jessica nodded and began to cry all over again.

Cathy shook her head. "Listen, girls," she said, "you come see me anytime you want to talk, OK?" She stared hard at Steven. "About *anything*," she added meaningfully, and she stalked away.

"Well, how'd we do?" Jessica asked. Cathy had disappeared around the corner. She dried off her pretend tears and grinned up at Steven. "You didn't mind the little improvising we did, did you?"

Steven could only squawk. "You promised!" he burst out.

"Yeah, well, you promised too," Jessica shot back, delighted to be on the winning side for a change. "What made you think you could lie to us and get away with it? We weren't born yesterday."

"What do you mean, lie?" Steven squeaked. "I *never* lie!"

"Yeah, right," Jessica said. "Didn't you know that Pete's cousins went back home?"

"They—did?" Steven's face froze. "Um—Pete didn't tell me that part," he stalled, buying time.

"*We* tried to," Elizabeth said. "But of course you wouldn't listen. Well, we saw through your game."

"Come on, Lizzie, let's get out of here," Jessica said. Smiling, she took her sister's hand. "Twins one, Steven nothing!" Elizabeth made a face as Jessica led her away. "But, Jess, we still don't have dates for the dance," she said dolefully. "Which means—"

The dance. Jessica had forgotten that part.

Quickly she covered her ears. She didn't want to hear about it.

All right, Steven thought. Fifteen minutes had gone by since he'd been so cruelly double-crossed, and he was still standing near the pharmacy door. *So I've been tricked, lied to, and played for a fool. So Cathy and I are, like, history.*

He sighed. It wasn't fun to admit it, exactly. But it was pretty clear now that this was the way things were. He patted down his hair. *Well, who cares?* he asked himself. *I've still got a girlfriend.*

Good old Jill. Just as well he'd waited to break up with her for real. Jill was popular and pretty, even if she was a little ditzy. She was a girlfriend that most guys would kill for. He could see the two of them at the street dance right now. Yeah. Dancing the night away, and as long as he didn't breathe too deeply around her, or listen too hard to what she said about nails and hair and skin care, well—

Face it, Wakefield, you're golden. Steven plastered a smile across his face. He had the girl of his dreams, and who cared about Cathy anyway? Jill was the one who truly loved him, truly needed him, truly *appreciated* him. Jill and only—

"Oh, Richard, you're so *funny!*" a voice cooed.

Steven's blood froze. There was something unsettlingly familiar about that voice.

Then an even more familiar smell floated to him through the air. Steven gulped and held his breath. He didn't need to turn around to know who it was.

Jill Hale.

Steven's heart sank like a heavy stone. Darting behind a nearby bush, he stared in shock as Jill came around the corner, arm in arm with—

With Richard Ferris.

"Yeah, well," Richard said modestly. He winked down at Jill. Not noticing Steven, he opened the pharmacy door and bowed gallantly. "After you, ma'am."

"Oh, Richard, you say the cleverest things!" Jill tittered. The door swung shut.

Steven blinked. Helplessly he leaned against the corner of the pharmacy wall.

Lied to, made a fool of, double-crossed—and now jilted.

His shoulders slumped forward, and he swallowed hard.

Things were getting truly serious.

"Life is completely unfair," Steven muttered to himself Tuesday evening. He was sprawled across his bed, facing the wall. No one else was home, and Steven decided he liked it that way.

Life *was* completely unfair. Through absolutely no fault of his own, he'd lost two girlfriends even though he was one of the coolest dudes he had personally ever met. *Yup.* Steven drummed his fingers on the bedspread. He'd had his pick, and they'd left him. Both of them. First Cathy, now Jill. *They must be brainwashed*, he decided. Cathy especially. Otherwise, why would she give up on him so easily? There wasn't any justice.

The doorbell rang.

Steven considered not answering it. He was in too much pain to talk to anybody. After what had happened today, he felt like he wanted to spend the rest of his life in bed. Steven rolled over and blinked up at the ceiling. "Go away," he said sourly to the model airplane hanging in his room. He bit his lip. The model airplane that Cathy had given him for his birthday—

The doorbell rang again.

Sighing, Steven swung his legs out of bed. There was always the chance that it might be Cathy, come to apologize. Or maybe Jill. At the moment, he'd take either one of them. Hopeful, he walked downstairs and flung open the door.

"Hey." Joe Howell nodded to Steven. "How you doing?"

Steven's only answer was a mournful chuckle. Joe was not exactly the person he'd wanted to see.

"That good, huh?" Joe asked brightly. "Well, I came to give you this." He handed Steven back his algebra book. "Sorry it took so long, but Cathy and me, we've been kind of getting to know each other, know what I mean?" He gave Steven a wink.

"Oh, great," Steven said. He wasn't about to invite Joe in, that was for sure. Hearing about what a great time Joe was having with Cathy was not high on his current "To Do" list.

"I mean, man, she is really something," Joe said. "I hate to say it, but I'm glad you guys stopped seeing eye to eye. I think maybe I'm a one-woman man." He laughed. "Can you imagine? Me! But Cathy's changed my outlook a lot, I'll tell you that. Hey, how's Jill?"

Steven chose not to answer this question. He bit his lip and stared at a point about three inches above Joe's left ear. *Cathy—Cathy—Cathy—* The name seemed to pound through his head. *I'm jealous,* he realized. *No, I'm not just jealous. I'm insanely jealous!*

"We couldn't get together tonight," Joe went on, "but I think I'm going to invite her to the street dance."

Steven sighed. In his mind's eye he could see

Cathy and Joe whirling around the dance floor. Just the way he and Cathy always used to. *Cathy— Cathy—* There was a lump in his throat. He remembered the way her hand had felt in his, the smile on her face, the way her eyes had shone when she looked at him. *And now I've gone and blown it.*

He set his jaw. If he couldn't have Cathy, he didn't want anybody else to have her either. "Listen, Joe," he said, his brain whizzing furiously, "there's something I gotta tell you about her. About Cath, I mean."

Joe raised his eyebrows. "What?"

"She's, like, two-faced," Steven said quickly before he could change his mind. "I don't know if she's been, you know, encouraging you," he went on, "but you need to know that she called me last night."

"She did not either." Joe shook his head violently.

"She did too," Steven snapped. What was another lie compared to all the ones he'd told already this week? Feeling a little guilty, he forged ahead. "She called me wanting to get back together."

"She—what?" Joe stared at Steven in astonishment.

"Like I said," Steven repeated weakly. "She called about getting back together." He devoutly wished she had too.

Joe shook his head. "If that's true, Wakefield, I'm—I'm through with her. I'm never taking her anywhere again, ever." He whirled in his tracks and stormed off. "And I'd advise you to leave her alone too!" he snarled over his shoulder.

Steven clutched the algebra book and watched him go, feeling just a little bit guilty. He wondered if he'd been entirely fair to Joe. Or to Cathy.

He sighed. Probably not. But what choice did he have?

"Hello!" Jessica's voice came over the answering machine. "We're-not-able-to-take-your-call-right-now," she said all in one breath, "but-if-you-leave-your-name-number-and-a-short-message, we'll-get-back-to-you. Thanks!"

Steven stared at the machine as it whirred. There was a click. He suspected he was being chicken by not answering the phone, but the way things were going, he was convinced it would only be bad news.

"Um, hi." Jill Hale's voice floated into the room. "This is for Steven?"

Steven's heart lifted.

"Anyway, this is Jill," Jill said. "I know I told you that I might go with you to the street dance. But I kind of changed my mind." She paused. "I'll be going with Richard instead."

Steven sat motionless, listening to Jill laugh. Only the laugh didn't sound like ringing bells anymore, he realized. *It sounds like a—like a cash register or something*, he thought bleakly.

"Over the last few days," Jill said in a satisfied voice, "Richard found out just how much he really missed me. So he wanted to get back together and—" She laughed again. "Well, thanks for every-thing, Steven. See you around."

There was a click.

"Thanks for everything!" Steven snarled. He felt completely empty. And what was worse, he felt like a fool.

Steven sucked in his breath. *Jill planned this*, he told himself. *She planned the whole thing.* She'd never been interested in *him*. Oh no. She'd just hung around with him to make Ferris jealous.

Yup, it all made sense now. He, Wakefield, was the designated goat. "Well, Ferris, you can have her and welcome to her!" he shouted. It felt good to shout and scream a little. "She's just a first-class jerk. The two-faced little—"

Abruptly Steven stopped yelling. The sudden si-lence rung in his ears. *Two-faced*, he thought with a sharp intake of breath. And he'd just gotten through calling Cathy two-faced.

Steven bit his lip. He had a sinking sensation in his stomach. *Cathy* wasn't two-faced; *Jill* was. That was clear. All at once, he regretted having told Joe that Cathy was two-faced. In fact, all at once he was regretting a lot of things.

He made a face. There were a lot of similarities between the way Jill had treated him and the way he had treated Cathy. He saw that now. He wished he could take back the whole last week, but, of course, he couldn't. So he'd just have to think of something else. In his mind he ticked off the people he'd managed to hurt or let down: Cathy, Joe, the twins. And most of all, himself.

He swallowed hard.

He didn't like what he was going to have to do.

But this time, he knew for *sure*, he didn't have a choice.

The front door banged about twenty minutes later. Steven tensed his body as he waited on the living room couch. With any luck, this would be his sisters.

"So now what?" came Jessica's tired voice.

Yes. Steven's heart raced. This wasn't going to be easy.

"I—I don't know," Elizabeth admitted. "I guess we could ask, like, Randy and Winston."

Steven couldn't help a grin. Not that he knew Randy Mason and Winston Eggface real well, but he couldn't see his sisters going out with them. Not even *Elizabeth.*

"Get real." Jessica walked into the living room.

"Dateless in Detroit?" Steven asked, trying to sound nonchalant. "I mean, Still Scheming in Sweet Valley?"

"Who wants to know?" Jessica asked, rolling her eyes and flopping down onto the couch.

Steven swallowed hard. He hated to get down on his knees to plead with his sisters, but his plan depended on them. "Listen, guys," he said urgently. "I really, *really* need your help. Seriously this time," he went on quickly before the girls could say anything. "And it's not what you think either. I don't want to get me and Cathy back together anymore; she's too good for me. What I want is—" He hesitated. It was awfully hard to explain. "I want to get her and Joe together. *Back* together."

Jessica gave a hollow laugh. "You're kidding, right?"

"It's the truth," Steven said earnestly, staring into her eyes.

For the last twenty minutes, he'd really thought about the situation. Cathy *was* too good for him, he'd decided. She deserved someone who would treat her right and not go around spreading lies about her. She deserved someone who appreciated her. Someone like Joe—his best buddy in the world, an honorable guy, a nice guy, a guy who really could be great with a girl like Cathy. "I've been kind of a jerk lately," he began, "and—"

"*What?*" Jessica exclaimed. "You're finally admitting the obvious?" She shook her head. "Call the loony bin," she suggested to Elizabeth. "Our brother is desperately ill."

"I'm serious!" Steven burst out. "I have to get Cathy and Joe back together again before it's too late!" He didn't like to think of how he had broken that romance up practically before it had even started—all because he was feeling jealous. *I totally blew it*, he thought. He'd considered only his own feelings, not anybody else's. And look what had happened. "And I need your help," he went on. "I really, really, *really* need your help."

Elizabeth sighed. "Why should we help you after everything that you've done?" she asked pointedly.

"Yeah, give us one good reason," Jessica said.

"Because—" Steven sighed. "Because I've, like, totally blown it with both of them. And Cathy likes you. She'll listen to you. If you tell her that I want her to get back together with *Joe*, then maybe she'll listen." He got down on his knees, feeling incredibly embarrassed. "Please?"

Jessica shook her head. "That's not what Elizabeth meant," she said. "She meant, what's in it for us?"

"What's in it for you?" Steven repeated. "Dates to the street dance, that's what."

"Oh, come *on*," Jessica said contemptuously, turning away.

"I mean it," Steven said doggedly. "I absolutely, one hundred percent guarantee you dates for the street dance on Friday. *Real* dates, not Winston Eggshell dates. And if I don't deliver, I'll—I'll—" He thought hard. "I'll do all your chores for the next week, no questions asked."

Jessica narrowed her eyes. "For the next month," she said.

"OK, the next month," Steven agreed quickly. He hoped his eyes radiated sincerity. "Promise."

"Who are these dates?" Elizabeth wanted to know.

Steven waved his hand in the air, trying to look confident. "You'll—really like these two mystery guys I have in mind. So how about it?"

Jessica stared at him. "All right," she said after a pause. "How about it, Elizabeth?"

Elizabeth sighed. "I can't believe we're doing this," she said gloomily. "You'd just better get us somebody good."

"Oh, I will," Steven assured her, scrambling delightedly to his feet.

He knew just where to look for the two guys he wanted.

And, after what he'd gone through the last few days, he knew just how to get them too.

Eleven

◇

"I can't believe we agreed to that deal with our so-called brother," Jessica said, her lips thin and pale.

Elizabeth blinked nervously and checked her watch. It was Friday evening, the street dance was scheduled to begin in less than twenty minutes, and they were sitting in the living room. Their "mystery dates" hadn't arrived. "I—I really thought he was telling the truth for a change," she said softly, wishing she could believe the best of her brother.

Jessica harrumphed. "After all we did for him too," she said bleakly. "And I don't even *want* a mystery date, I want—" She stopped abruptly.

"I know," Elizabeth said, nodding. *She really wants to go with Aaron, and I really want to go with Todd. But they're at the basketball game.*

"If Steven doesn't come through, I will personally kill him," Jessica warned.

"Let's give it a few more minutes," Elizabeth
suggested. She shifted uncomfortably in her chair,
hoping that she wouldn't have to go change her
nice blue skirt for an outfit that matched her sister's. "Anyway, I don't know if you can say we
held up our end of the bargain either," she admitted. "We promised to help him get Cathy and Joe
together, and—"

The doorbell rang.

"Coming!" Jessica shouted, getting up from her
seat in such a hurry that her chair went flying. "It's
probably just somebody selling Girl Scout cookies,"
she hissed over her shoulder.

"Probably," Elizabeth agreed, but she was hoping against hope that it would be two guys. Two incredibly cute guys.

Jessica threw open the door.

Elizabeth's jaw dropped open.

There, on the front porch, dressed in their nicest
clothes, stood Aaron Dallas and Todd Wilkins.

"Wh-what are *you* doing here?" Jessica demanded. Her throat felt tight, and her head was
pounding, and she absolutely could not breathe.
She stared in astonishment from Aaron to Todd
and back. "You're—you're supposed to be playing
basketball."

Aaron bowed low and held out a bouquet of

flowers. Mechanically, Jessica took them. "We heard you two had, like, a couple of hot dates for the evening," he said, raising an eyebrow.

Jessica could only stare. "But—but—" Her mind reeled.

"Well, how about breaking those dates and going to the street dance with us?" Todd asked. He stood awkwardly in the doorway and aimed a shy grin at Elizabeth.

· Jessica found her voice at last. "But what about—you know, the basketball game?"

"Basketball game?" Aaron turned to Todd, frowning. "Was there a basketball game?"

"*Some* people are going to a basketball game," Todd explained, a smile curving around his lips. "Guys like Jake Hamilton and Denny Jacobson. But we can play basketball any old time." He handed Elizabeth a bouquet too.

"Yeah," Aaron broke in. "But it's not every day we can take two lovely young ladies to a dance. We just figured, you know, the dance was more important." He took a quick nervous glance over his shoulder. "So, um, how about it? Want to go?"

"Yeah, break those mystery dates, huh?" Todd asked, drumming his fingers against the side of the house.

Jessica bit her lip. She didn't understand this at all. But who was she to complain?

"You're on!" she exclaimed.

*   *   *

Steven watched from the bushes as Jessica and Aaron sauntered down the front walk arm in arm, followed a moment later by Todd and Elizabeth. He breathed a sigh of relief. *Good.*

He'd known those guys would come through for him. All he'd had to do was whisper the magic words into their heads: "Mystery Date." *Yup*, he told himself, *just one little hint that some other guy might be interested, and they went right to the coach and asked to be excused from the Glenwood game.* He grinned, remembering how he'd talked so earnestly Thursday afternoon with Dallas. "I'm telling you, man," he'd said, lying through his teeth, "there's this guy who's been calling Jessica, like, every night." Funny how that had been all it had taken. Jealousy was strong stuff, all right. Which he well knew by now.

Oh boy, did he ever know that by now.

"I have to say I'm pretty surprised," Elizabeth was saying primly as they disappeared down the sidewalk toward the street dance. "I mean, I was all set for this *other* guy showing up."

Todd grimaced. "I guess we showed up just in time."

Steven wondered if the twins knew what he'd been up to. Probably not. And it didn't matter anyway. As long as they'd kept up their end of the deal. As long as they'd gotten Joe and Cathy back together. In a minute he'd head over to the street dance, just to make sure. He winced, thinking about seeing Cathy and Joe holding hands, hugging, maybe even kissing.

Cruel and unusual punishment. But he deserved it. That was for sure.

Slowly Steven rose to his feet and stretched. Hiding in the bushes was not an activity designed for basketball players, he decided. Every muscle ached.

Cathy, he thought bleakly, remembering once when Cathy had gently massaged his neck after he'd strained it during a game.

Steven swallowed hard. He missed her terribly.

But she was somebody else's girl now.

"Jessica?" Janet gasped. She looked up and down across the dance floor, her jaw dropping open in astonishment. "What are *they* doing here?"

Jessica felt a surge of triumph. "Hi, Janet," she said.

"Denny. Where's Denny?" Janet demanded, pointing a finger straight at Aaron. "If *you're* here, where's *Denny?*"

Aaron grinned and put a protective hand on Jessica's arm. "At the game," he said simply.

"But why aren't you and Todd—" Janet put her hand to her mouth.

"Excuse us, *please*," Aaron said, steering Jessica out into the sea of dancers.

Jessica sighed with relief and turned away from Janet. "I'm really glad you showed up when you did," she said mischievously.

Aaron coughed. "Yeah. I was, um, glad you hadn't left already," he told her shyly. "I was worried that—" He coughed again. "Well. Never mind."

Jessica's heart soared. He really did care after all. As the music changed to a slow dance, her eyes swept around the street. Aaron really had abandoned the game, she could tell. It hadn't been canceled or anything. The only middle-school guys she could see were Randy and a few of his nerdy friends. And Winston, doing his gargoyle imitations on the edge of the curb.

Jessica's eyes swept along as Aaron pulled her tighter. There was the band, with Joe doing a guitar solo. And there, on the other side of the street, was Cathy.

She narrowed her eyes, wondering where her brother was.

"So," Aaron muttered into her hair, "who was the mystery guy anyway?"

Jessica didn't know, but on the whole she decided she didn't care either. Aaron was worth six mystery dates. "Oh, I think that'll just have to be my secret," she said, burrowing further into Aaron's arms.

"Todd?" Elizabeth asked nervously.

Todd's grip tightened on Elizabeth's hand. "What?"

Elizabeth swallowed hard. Not that she was really worried or anything, but she really had to know. "Todd?" she asked again over the sound of the music. "Are you, like, interested in anybody else? In, say, Cammi Adams or somebody?"

"Cammi Adams?" Todd frowned. "Cammi *Adams?* Cammi's a nice kid, but—why would I be interested in Cammi Adams?"

Elizabeth bit back a grin. "Oh—no reason," she said quickly. "I was just—wondering."

Nervously, Steven looked into the swirl of dancers. He'd just arrived at the dance and he was standing near the curb. He knew it would be incredibly painful to see Joe and Cathy with their arms around each other, but he also knew that was best for both his friends. Taking a deep breath, he looked at Joe.

Only—Joe was sitting all alone, resting his fingers, his guitar at his side. And Cathy was nowhere around.

Worried, Steven scanned the rest of the crowd. After an anxious minute he saw Cathy, talking with some of her friends on the other side of the street.

Steven felt his fists clench and unclench. "Why, those double-crossing little rats!" he snarled, kicking a pebble. Here he'd gone to all this trouble to get his sisters partners for the dance, and they hadn't lifted a finger to get Cathy and Joe back together.

The music hit a final chord. Joe picked up the mike, and his voice boomed across the street. "Two beautiful young ladies," he announced, "who just happen to look very much alike, have requested a special song."

Then don't play it, Steven urged Joe silently, knowing exactly who those "two young ladies" were. He absolutely could not believe it. *Try to be nice, just once in your life, and look what happens!* he thought.

"But first," Joe continued, "I have an important announcement."

Jessica frowned. What could be more important, she wondered, than the song she and Elizabeth had asked the band to—

"Those two young ladies," Joe said, his lips curving into a grin, "have arrived at this dance with dates."

You got that right, Jessica thought, smiling at Aaron.

"*Which* a certain person didn't think they could," Joe went on meaningfully. "So that certain person has lost a certain bet which she was sure she was going to win. And now she has something she really wants to say to all of you."

"Yay, Janet!" Jessica called. Now she understood what Joe was up to. She whistled and clapped her hands.

"Presenting—my little sister!" Joe called out, holding the microphone toward Janet.

"Jan-et! Jan-et!" Jessica chanted. She was going to enjoy this moment. "Jan-et! Jan-et!"

Janet approached the microphone, cheeks flaming. "I just wanted to say," she began, gritting her teeth, "that my brother's band is—" Her voice trailed off.

"Say it," Aaron yelled. "Don't be shy."

Joe grabbed the microphone back. "Louder," he teased. "We can't hear you!"

Janet blushed even more. "My brother's band is better than Johnny Buck's!" she yelled.

"You've heard it from our toughest critic," Joe observed as Janet ran off quickly. "Ladies and gentlemen, a round of applause, please, for Miss Janet Howell, a lady who tells it like it is!"

Jessica beamed and clapped as ferociously as she could.

She even almost felt a little tiny bit sorry for Janet.

Almost!

"Wanna see Gargoyle the Fifth?" Winston asked hopefully. He nudged a hat toward Steven.

Steven glanced down and saw three coins at the bottom of the hat. He wasn't in the mood for this. He wasn't even close to being in the mood for this. Not even after watching Janet be totally embarrassed. Angrily, he kicked the hat away.

"Hey," Winston said reproachfully.

"And now," Joe said, grinning like a game-show host, "here's that very special song, sent out to two very special people who are here tonight." He set the mike down, signaled to the other musicians, and led straight into—

Into—

Steven's heart lurched as he recognized the opening chords of "You and Me." *Our song,* he told himself dismally. *Cathy's and mine. And now I've lost her,* he reminded himself, feeling more miserable than he could ever remember. He closed his eyes, humming along in spite of himself. "You and me," he sang softly. "Me and you. Never more feeling blue—"

He bit his lip. It was all he could do to keep from breaking down and crying. An infinite sadness overwhelmed him. In his mind he could see Cathy's smile and Cathy's sparkling eyes, hear Cathy's laugh, feel the brush of Cathy's hand against his arm. *Why does Howell have to play that song?* he thought angrily, opening his eyes and blinking back tears. *Doesn't he know what he's doing to—*

His jaw dropped open. There in front of him stood Cathy. The *real* Cathy, not an imaginary one. Steven blinked.

"Hi, Steven," Cathy said, smiling up at him with that grin he knew so well. Her hand reached out to clasp his.

"Want to dance?"

"But—but what about Joe?" Steven asked, resisting the urge to fall into Cathy's arms right there on the spot.

Cathy laughed. "Joe's just a very good friend," she told him. "And he helped me a lot."

"He—what?" Steven's head spun. He had the sudden feeling that there was a lot going on that he didn't quite understand.

"I made up my mind that I didn't want to lose you," Cathy said, reaching up to pick a stray hair out of Steven's eye. "So I used one of the oldest tricks in the book, I admit it." She smiled. "Jealousy! Joe was just putting on an act when he came over to your house and told you he was interested."

"He was?" Steven asked incredulously. He held Cathy's hand a little tighter. "He didn't—he didn't sound like he was acting."

"Well, he was," Cathy assured him. "He's a pretty good actor, Joe is. And, you know, he really wants to see us together too."

Steven swallowed hard. "But—how about when I said you were, um—" He didn't want to say "two-faced." "Joe stomped out and said—well, he sure looked angry."

"All an act," Cathy teased him. "And that was when I knew I was really getting to you! So how about it, Steven? Want to dance?"

Steven took a quick look over at the band. Joe was playing along, studiously ignoring him and Cathy. "And the twins?" he wanted to know, feeling angry all over again. "I made a deal with them and—"

"Let's just say a lot of people thought you needed to be taught a lesson, Steven," Cathy interrupted. She put her arm through his. A jolt of energy seemed to pass through his body. "They came to me, just like you asked them to."

"They did?" Steven frowned. He hadn't expected that.

Cathy smiled. "They didn't ask me to get back together with Joe," she told him. "They told me that was what you wanted, but they asked me not to do it. They asked me to get back together with *you*."

"They did?" Steven asked stupidly.

"Yup. They said that *they* didn't want to lose me. It wasn't because they liked you so much." Cathy laughed. "In fact, they said you were a real creep. But because they liked me."

Steven's mouth felt dry. In the background he dimly heard Joe's lead guitar strumming the melody. "You and me, me and you. Not just one, just us two . . ."

"But the important thing is that you finally started looking out for my happiness," Cathy said, looking deep into Steven's eyes. "Even if that happiness was with another guy. And that was what convinced me I was doing the right thing by trying to get back together with you."

Steven swallowed. "You mean—"

"Yup," Cathy said, laying a finger gently on his lips. "I think you've finally learned your lesson, Stevie boy. You've learned to respect other people's feelings."

"Hey, will you two dance already?" Joe's voice rang out over the music.

Steven's heart felt like bursting. "That's me, sensitive and a good listener," he said as he steered Cathy into the middle of the street. "From now on, I promise I'll think about your feelings.

And everybody else's too," he added, reminding himself to thank Joe. Maybe even the twins.

The music swelled. "You and me," Steven sang in a husky voice, enveloping Cathy to his chest. "Me and you. How I love what you do . . ."

Cathy stirred and nestled closer to Steven's shoulder. "Think we could, like, get back together again?" she asked.

Steven couldn't speak. He held Cathy tight and stroked her back. *This is what I need,* he told himself. He felt absolutely at peace. *What an awful week. But it's turned out all right.*

"I'll take that as a yes," Cathy said jokingly when Steven didn't say a word.

Steven stared down at Cathy. What a lucky guy he was. "'You and me,'" he sang along with the final chorus, gently rocking in place with Cathy in his arms.

"'Me and you,'" Cathy sang back.

Steven grinned. Holding each other tight, they sang the last line together: "Happy all our lives through—me and you."

The music died away into the night air. As the last chord rippled out of Joe's guitar and the audience started to clap, Steven bent down to Cathy.

And their lips met in a kiss.

"What a miserable day," Jessica sighed, looking out at the streams of rain pelting out of the sky.

Elizabeth nodded. "At least it waited till after

the street dance. Hey, look!" Elizabeth grabbed her sister's shoulder. "Isn't that a rainbow?"

Jessica stared off into the distance. There was the dim outline of a rainbow, all right, floating just off the earth as if suspended in midair.

"That is *so* beautiful," Elizabeth murmured. "I wonder what's at the end of it?"

"The ground, doofus," Jessica snapped.

Elizabeth shook her head. "That's not what I meant, Jess. I wasn't talking about real life. Isn't there some old legend about leprechauns and pots of gold and stuff like that?" Elizabeth stared off at the rainbow again, and her eyes shone.

Leprechauns. Jessica snorted. She was about to make a cutting retort when suddenly she realized that her sister had mentioned something else besides little green people.

"A pot of gold?" she asked slowly.

Her heart thudded in her chest.

Hmm. This had possibilities.

Will Jessica find a pot of gold? Find out in Sweet Valley Twins 105, JESSICA'S LUCKY MILLIONS.

Bantam Books in the SWEET VALLEY TWINS series.
Ask your bookseller for the books you have missed.

SIGN UP FOR THE SWEET VALLEY HIGH® FAN CLUB!

Hey, girls! Get all the gossip on Sweet Valley High's® most popular teenagers when you join our fantastic Fan Club! As a member, you'll get all of this really cool stuff:

- Membership Card with your own personal Fan Club ID number
- A Sweet Valley High® Secret Treasure Box
- Sweet Valley High® Stationery
- Official Fan Club Pencil (for secret note writing!)
- Three Bookmarks
- A "Members Only" Door Hanger
- Two Skeins of J. & P. Coats® Embroidery Floss with flower barrette instruction leaflet
- Two editions of *The Oracle* newsletter
- Plus exclusive Sweet Valley High® product offers, special savings, contests, and much more!

- -

Be the first to find out what Jessica & Elizabeth Wakefield are up to by joining the Sweet Valley High® Fan Club for the one-year membership fee of only $6.25 each for U.S. residents, $8.25 for Canadian residents (U.S. currency). Includes shipping & handling.

Send a check or money order (do not send cash) made payable to "Sweet Valley High® Fan Club" along with this form to:

SWEET VALLEY HIGH® FAN CLUB, BOX 3919-B, SCHAUMBURG, IL 60168-3919

NAME_____

(Please print clearly)

ADDRESS_____

CITY_____ STATE _____ ZIP_____

(Required)

AGE _____ BIRTHDAY_____ /_____ /_____